# LAST CHANCE BRIDE

## REDEMPTION SERIES BOOK 1

### CASSIE MALONE

LIVE LIFE FULLY MEDIA

# 1

As the evening shadows grew long, Hazel Young hid in the dark alley behind Pritchard's Tavern. On the main avenue, street lamps flickered, but in the faded light of the dim alleyway, her worn black cloak provided the perfect camouflage. Only a desperate woman would venture near such an establishment, overrun with drunkards and thieves. Sadly, that's what she was —desperate.

Penniless and unemployed, she'd scoured the streets of Charleston for weeks in search of any job she could find. Times were tough, and work was scarce. She was turned away at every doorstep, and in one case, chased by a toothless bloodhound. The war ended two years ago, but tensions between coloreds and whites were still thick enough to cut with a hatchet. Because of her mixed-race appearance, some folks didn't even give her a chance to open her mouth before they slammed the back door in her face. It seemed about the only thing she was good for was cleaning wounds and patching up soldiers.

She shuddered. She'd seen enough of that working as a nurse in the filthy battlefield hospitals. She was sick of the sight of blood. Tired of the sound of musket fire. Disgusted by the stench of gangrene and infections. Wild mustangs couldn't drag her back.

Abruptly, the back door of the tavern burst open. Bright light and raucous conversation spilled out, along with a group of men. Three males stumbled out, carting a fourth. One held him by the scruff of his collar. The other two clasped his long legs. Even in the dark, she could see the man they carried was well dressed. White, ruffled cuffs peeked beneath the sleeves of his tailcoat. He was a gentleman, but the others didn't seem to care. They dumped him unceremoniously upon the muddy cobblestones.

"That'll teach you to cheat at cards!" one of the men growled.

"Black hearted scoundrel," a shorter, chubby man spat. The necklace of expletives he strung together made her cheeks burn.

The third man said nothing, but his thick boot delivered a swift kick to the gentleman's midsection.

Then the attackers lumbered back inside the tavern, leaving their victim sprawled on his stomach on the ground. The man's anguished groan lured her from her hiding spot. Her training as a nurse wouldn't allow her to abandon a person in need of medical attention. She scurried to his side, careful not to get her only pair of slippers soaked in the nearby puddles.

"Sir, are you hurt?"

The man's only reply was more groaning. The acrid smell of stale ale and urine assaulted her nostrils. She covered her nose with her handkerchief. The poor fool was probably drunk. She had no business being here. Unchaperoned. In the dark. With a stranger. Nonetheless, she squatted beside him and rolled him onto his back.

She gasped at the grotesque red stain soiling his stark, white shirt. Gentlemen usually wore vests. His was missing.

"Stabbed..." he murmured.

"Dear Lord!" She forced back a wave of panic. She'd seen worse than this in the makeshift tents of the Confederate hospitals. She simply hadn't expected to encounter such violence in civilians. She shook her head. A knife wound to the belly could be fatal. She tugged at the man's cravat, loosening the knot so he could breathe. By the sound of his labored wheezing, he didn't have much longer on this earth. All she could do was make his final moments as comfortable as possible.

"Poc...pocket..." His mouth gaped open, but no other words came out.

Her gaze slid to the pockets of his coat. "You want me to get something out of your pocket?" She looked at him for confirmation, but his eyes were closed. The man had said *pocket*, hadn't he? What was in there? Why did he want her to look inside?

She let out a long breath. She took issue with his request. She was no thief. Under normal circumstances, she would never rifle through a man's pockets — no matter how hungry she was.

*These are not normal circumstances.*

Her conscience needled her. Yet this was hardly the time or place to argue with herself. Someone could come along and find her hunched over this white man in this dark alley. They might think she'd killed him. Or worse yet, the men from the tavern could return at any moment. Either way, she'd be in quite a pickle. She needed to make a decision fast.

A coyote howled in the distance, spurring her to action. Pritchard's was on the outskirts of town, purposely constructed away from the prying eyes of authorities and nosey wives. Unfortunately, wild animals were a consequence of its remote location.

She dug into the man's left coat pocket.

Then his right.

Both were empty.

Why the heck had he told her to search his pockets if there was nothing in there but lint? She huffed in irritation. The best thing to do was button up his coat and leave him here for someone else to find him. Someone with more power and influence than her. Someone who would make sure he got a proper burial. Someone who had more than two coins to rub together.

She reached for his collar, intent on straightening his coat and placing him in a respectful casket pose. Her fingers brushed across something stiff beneath the fine fabric. A folded piece of parchment sticking out of his inside lapel pocket caught her attention. It felt wrong to search through his personal effects, but he had told her to look in his pocket, hadn't he? Maybe this was the pocket he spoke of.

She unfolded the paper. Thank goodness she knew how to read. Born to a black man and a white woman, nursing wasn't the only talent she possessed. Her father descended from a long line of medicine men in Africa. Slavers captured him not far from his village when he was only fifteen, but he never forgot the knowledge of his forefathers. He was fortunate to earn his freedom. When he met her mother, the daughter of a local physician, they discovered they had more in common than an initial spark of attraction.

She'd learned so much from each of her parents, including how to read and write.

Sadly, they were both dead now.

She blinked back tears as she tried to focus on the words in the letter. She scanned the plain paper with the bold script. She could tell it was a man's handwriting. Women wrote in dainty loops and flowing lines. This penmanship was crude and rugged. The t's were crossed like a man wielding a sword. The i's were dotted with rough stabs, the pen nearly puncturing the paper in some places. Whoever had written this letter was either an angry man or someone in a hurry.

As her eyes darted across the message, her jaw dropped. Apparently, the gentleman at her feet was a solicitor. The letter was from a client who'd paid him to find a mail order bride. The ticket for the woman's transport was waiting now at the train station.

*Ticket to where?*

She found her answer in the next lines of the letter. Daniel Webster, the owner of the Last Chance Ranch in Redemption, Montana requested that Leonard Potts, Esquire send his bride immediately. Hazel's heart ricocheted against her ribcage. Last chance? Redemption? Those were words she knew all too well.

"Sir, why did you want me to see this?"

When the man didn't reply, she bent her head low, placing her ear near his mouth. More questions would be useless. He was dead.

She rocked back on her heels, clutching the mysterious letter in her trembling hands. What was she supposed to do with this information? Perhaps it was a sign from God. Maybe this man wasn't a man at all. Maybe he was an angel, sent to give her a chance to start a new life.

*Don't be daft! Why would an angel take the form of a drunkard?*

Many times in the Bible, angels appeared as messengers, disguised as ordinary people. But Satan had also disguised himself as a snake in the Garden of Eden. What if this was a temptation she should not surrender to? She could be stealing someone's blessing by taking this letter. What of the woman Daniel Webster inquired about? Had Mr. Potts already selected someone? Did he have any prospects lined up for the rancher?

*I could be the very prospect he needs.*

No sooner than she'd formed the thought she dismissed it. She couldn't marry a complete stranger! Her parents had married for love. She wanted that same love. She'd seen the way her daddy gazed at her mama with adoration in his eyes. The kind way he'd treated her. The gentle way he'd spoken to her. She'd also seen how much her mama cherished her daddy. How she showed her love through the meals she cooked and the care she took mending his clothes. Mama did everything in her power to convey her devotion, even nursing him through the raging fever that eventually killed him.

Not even death could stop their love. When daddy died, a part of mama died with him. Even though she lived for six more years until her accidental death, she wasn't the same woman. Her eyes didn't have the same twinkle. Her laugh didn't have the same enthusiasm. It was sure hard to see her mama's vibrant personality fade, but Hazel still wanted that kind of love. The all-consuming, 'make you count your blessings' kind of love.

Could Mr. Webster give her that? She sincerely doubted it. He was probably a rough rancher looking for a woman to serve not only as his wife, but his maid and cook as well.

She let out a deep breath. She had no other options. She was twenty years old. Other women her age had resorted to making a living on their backs—a wretched existence. It would be unchristian to judge them, so she didn't. But that would never be the life for her.

The sound of footsteps shuffling behind the door sent a jolt of fear through her. She sprang to her feet and rushed back to her hiding spot. A plump woman with rosy cheeks and a stained apron bustled through the door. When she saw the lump of well-dressed flesh on the ground, she called out, "Carl, we got another souse back here!"

Within moments, the brawny frame of a man Hazel could only assume was Carl ducked through the doorway. He nudged the body with his the toe of his massive boot. The flap of Mr. Potts' coat slipped away, revealing the hideous bloodstain. Carl frowned. "He ain't drunk, Ma. He's dead."

"Well, git him outta here." The woman turned to leave, but stopped midstride. "Wait. Check his pockets."

Carl hunkered down and fished through Mr. Potts' pockets.

The woman spat when her son's meaty hands came up with nothing. "Another high roller without a red cent to his name. As usual, I'm left to clean up the mess."

Once again, Hazel was shocked by these people's callous disregard for life. She wondered if the war had hardened the woman or if she was already bitter and unfeeling before Union troops destroyed the city.

Carl nodded, plucked the body off the ground, and slung it over his shoulder as though it weighed no more than a sack of flour.

The woman's suspicious eyes flickered to and fro, scanning the alley.

Hazel shrank against a brick wall, glad she couldn't be seen. She fingered the letter she'd tucked into the deep pockets of her cloak. Thank God, she'd gotten the most valuable asset Mr. Potts owned—a ticket to a better life. She hurried away, swallowed by the dark shadows of the night. She had a train to catch.

## 2

"Gimme my dolly!"

"It's mine now!"

Childish laughter followed by a high-pitched shriek punctured the morning silence.

"May! June! March! August! Let's get going. Time's a wastin'."

Daniel Webster shoved his head beneath the down feather pillow, desperate to block out the cacophony of children's voices mingling with his father's gruff commands. The old man wasn't reciting the months of the calendar. He was issuing his morning orders. Reining his grandkids was like corralling cats.

Suddenly, the door to Daniel's spacious bedroom burst open. "Uncle Daniel! March stole dolly. Make him give her back."

He'd clung to the last vestiges of slumber like a man holding onto a buoy in a storm. It was no use. He wasn't going to get anymore sleep today. He cracked an eye open to see a mop of blonde curls flounce into the room. The owner's denim blue eyes filled with tears. A pout tugged at her tiny lips. Of course, she wasn't really crying. This was a performance she put on at least once a day to get her way. With a cherub face and a willful attitude, no one could resist six-year-old, May Webster for long.

He tried to feign sleep, but she wasn't fooled. "Uncle Daniel! I know you ain't sleepin'."

She scampered barefoot across the large, braided rug and stood by his bed, her chin barely reaching the top of the massive mattress. The girl was the spitting image of her mama, Caroline. His heart wrenched just thinking about the vibrant redhead who'd died a year ago. If only she'd survived. If only she had been his wife instead of another man's, maybe this is what their child would've looked like. He swallowed feelings of resentment. Wishing wouldn't make it so. Nothing could bring Caroline back. All he had now were bittersweet memories and the four children she left behind.

He slid a bare arm from beneath the heavy patchwork quilt and pulled May closer. "What have you done to make March steal your doll?"

"Nuthin'. He's just mean and ornery—like Grandpa."

Her eight-year-old brother, March, might be as stubborn as an old mule. But Grandpa, also known as Levi Webster, Daniel's father, was far from it. In fact, he was useless when it came to disciplining the children. Each one of them had the old man wrapped around their little fingers. That was part of the reason they'd been allowed to run roughshod over everything, including this house.

May coughed, a tiny rattle of phlegm caught in her throat. "Sounds like someone needs some medicine."

"No!" she protested. "I don't want no nasty medicine! I want dolly."

She slipped from his hold like a greased up piglet. "All

right," he relented. "Give me some privacy to get dressed. I'll be downstairs in a few minutes and I'll get your doll back."

Fake tears forgotten, she darted out of the room, slamming the door behind her. That was how May operated. She was the youngest of the family, but she was also the loudest. He rose from his comfortable mattress and pulled on the pair of trousers he'd abandoned at the foot of his bed last night. After helping his prize cow, Nellie, through a backward birth, he was exhausted. He'd spent half the evening in the barn, up to his elbows in afterbirth and muck, trying to turn the calf so it could come out headfirst, front feet extended. He finally made it back to the house well past eleven o'clock. It was a wonder he hadn't fallen asleep with his boots on.

He splashed tepid water from the porcelain bowl of his washstand onto his face. Toweling off, he took one glance in the mirror and grimaced. His five o'clock shadow had turned into a midnight silhouette. He rubbed a calloused palm over the stubble on his jaw. Surely, he had time for a quick shave. A squeal of noises followed by stomping on the hardwood floors below told him otherwise. His personal grooming would have to wait.

He struggled into last night's stale shirt, caked with the scent of musk and horseflesh. Not bothering with socks, he trotted barefoot downstairs to investigate the ruckus. Following the voices through the parlor, he skidded to a stop at the open kitchen door. He should be used to the morning flurry of activity, but it always shocked his senses.

Four unsupervised children raced around the large room. Dirty plates, bowls, and glasses half-filled with milk cluttered the large wooden table that dominated the kitchen. His gaze flew to the new stove he'd purchased only last month after March had put a firecracker in the oven.

Cast iron skillets littered the burners now, the evidence of something black and charcoaled encrusted to their bottoms. The smell of scorched food stung the air. Judging from the broken eggshells on the floor, it was obvious someone had attempted to make bacon and eggs.

"I can't find my shoe!" ten-year-old, June zoomed past. The clip clop rhythm of her bare left foot smacking the floor alongside her booted right foot made her sound like a horse that had thrown a shoe.

Her brother, August, yanked her ponytail as she ran. At twelve, he was the oldest of the brood. With dark hair and a budding muscular build, he was quickly outgrowing child-hood. "Hey Unc!" he called, when he noticed Daniel standing at the threshold. "We just finished breakfast. Sorry we didn't make none for ya." A mischievous grin split his dimpled cheeks.

"Yeah," March added in his sullen voice. "Besides, you never eat no breakfast any way."

Daniel cringed at the boys' bad grammar. Every day he corrected the children. And every day they continued to abuse the English language. Bad habits were hard to break.

June galloped by and smacked August on the back of his head. "Tag! You're it!" She fled from the room before her brother could catch her.

August, June, March, and May. Daniel's brother, Mark, and his wife, Caroline had an awful sense of humor—naming their children for the month in which Caroline had given birth. But names were the least of these kids' prob-lems. Orphaned when their parents died in a tragic accident last year, the quartet was an unruly group of little hellions. Though he hadn't been on good terms with Mark and Caro-line when they died, he could never turn their children out into the streets. He was all they had.

"My dolly!" May screeched.

March sprinted for the door, but Daniel clapped a firm hand on the boy's slender shoulder. "Give your sister her doll, boy."

March yanked the ragdoll from the back pocket of his jeans, gave it a punch in the face, and then threw it to August. When May ran to August to get the doll, he threw it back to March, playing a cruel game of *keep away* from their little sister.

Daniel intercepted the doll and gave it to May. She rewarded him with a snaggletooth grin.

"Hey, when did you lose a tooth?" he asked her.

"It was already loose," March sneered. "So, I just helped it along."

"He knocked it out, last night!" May accused.

Daniel glared in March's direction. "Boy—"

Daniel's father, Levi, hobbled into the room, leaning heavily on the scarred wood of his cane. "You young'uns get in that wagon so I can take you to school. Come on or we'll be late."

The gang rushed out, a whirlwind of book satchels and scuffles. Daniel stared at the mess they'd left behind. "I miss Evening Sun."

"Me too. But I'm pretty sure she doesn't miss us."

Evening Sun was their previous maid. The sweet Chippewa widow couldn't handle the demands of the brood, so she left after only two months. Work was plentiful in Redemption, and someone with her cooking skills was eagerly scooped up. She didn't have to deal with what she'd referred to as 'cruel and unusual punishment.' Daniel sighed. So far, he'd lost two housekeepers and three cooks to the brood's bad behavior.

"Why are you taking the children to school?" he asked his father. "Where is Nicolai?"

"His wife went into labor early this morning. He's with her."

Nicolai was one of his trusted ranch hands who got the unenviable task of driving the Webster children to school each morning. "Seems everyone is having a baby nowadays." That was one thing this town was never short on. Maybe one day all the babies would grow up to be girls and they'd finally have enough women in this town to tilt the population in the men's favor.

"What happened to you last night?" his father asked.

Daniel began clearing away the dirty dishes. There was nowhere to put them, since two turtles were camped out in the sink. It was hard to know which of the children had put them there. "Pa, you know I was down at the stables with Nelly."

"You could have let one of the other men handle that."

"Nelly is special to me. She's getting on in age, and her last two pregnancies were difficult. I wanted to be there to make sure everything turned out all right."

"You need to spend less time in the cow pens and more time with these young'uns. You're never here anymore."

"Somebody's gotta run the ranch."

"You can't outrun your memories, son."

Their gazes locked. Daniel choked back a wave of emotion. He didn't want to think about sweet Caroline or how he felt when she'd left him for another man — his own brother.

Pa shoved his free hand into the pocket of his worn, dusty dungarees. "Their deaths were hard on me, too. Since I came to Montana I've lost a wife, a son, and a daughter-in-law. Death is part of life. We've got to go on living."

"I *am* living." Frustrated, he set the dirty dishes back on the table.

"If you call treading water, living. You're in over your head, son. These children need a firm hand."

"I'm taking care of that today."

"How? You found a governess for all of 'em?"

"No."

Daniel had known for some time he needed the type of help only a female could give. Neither he nor Pa had been lucky with women. His parents migrated to Redemption from Philadelphia twenty-eight years ago. His mother, Geraldine, was a beautiful, wealthy debutant. The only thing her money couldn't buy was good health. Desperate to save her life, Levi Webster brought her west, where the air was reportedly better for her frail lungs.

The two made it safely, along with their young boys. The journey wasn't the problem. Geraldine's health was. She died a year after arriving, a week before Daniel's sixth birthday. Mark, three years older, had taken it a lot harder. Pa never remarried. Having no reason to return back east, he and his sons threw themselves into creating the Last Chance Ranch.

Daniel thought he would marry. He courted Caroline for months before he brought her to the ranch to meet his brother and father. He had wanted their blessing before he proposed to her. Wanted to be sure they would be amenable to his moving her into their home.

He had not expected Caroline and Mark to fall in love at first site. Their attraction was instantaneous and it was as if he no longer existed in her eyes. In the years since, Daniel was determined to never lose his heart to a woman again. Never to be so vulnerable. He did think a wife would be practical, however. The ranch could certainly use the female touch, as could the children.

With long days and endless work, Daniel had precious little time to find a wife, and even less time to court a woman. He'd heard some of the men in town talk about mail order brides. He figured why not give it a try? Just like the name of their ranch, this could be his last chance, too.

"I found a wife, Pa. A mail order bride. I'm picking her up from the station today."

He thought his father would balk at the idea, but he didn't. The old man nodded. "Best decision you've made all year."

Daniel scoffed. "The moment she gets a look at this place, she'll probably hightail it right back to the train station."

"It's up to you to make her stay. Show her how much we need her. And son, don't mess it up. The future of these children is in your hands."

"Thanks for the vote of confidence," Daniel grumbled.

His pa ambled to the door. "Don't forget to wear a suit."

"I'm not wearing a suit, Pa. I don't even own one."

Levi Webster paused and tossed him a scowl. "You're the richest man in the county. Why on earth don't you have a suit?"

"People I do business with don't give a hoot what I wear. All they care about is that I create jobs and make money for this town."

"Fine. If that's the first impression you want to make on your new bride, go ahead." He reached the open door." And for God's sake, shave them whiskers. You can't meet the woman looking like a grizzly bear!"

## 3

D aniel sat in his buckboard across the street from the train depot. He tugged at the stiff collar of his clean, cotton shirt. He'd taken Pa's advice and worn a suit coat. Just something he found wedged in the back of his armoire. But instead of the matching suit pants, he'd worn his canvas trousers. And his Stetson. His hat was one thing he wasn't getting rid of. He glanced down at his spit-shined boots. This was as presentable as he was going to get. He still had work to do back on the ranch. Even though he employed a team of six men, he liked being there to keep an eye on things. The ranch wasn't going to run itself.

His family owned two hundred acres of land. Green pastures. Bubbling brooks of clear spring water. Wide open spaces. He had a life most men would envy. Money. Respect. Power. All that was missing was a woman to share it. He glanced at his pocket watch. The train was late. The nervous thump of his heart quickened to an erratic beating. What if the woman didn't come? What if she'd changed her mind? What if Leonard Potts hadn't found anyone suitable? He hadn't heard from the lawyer in over a week, but today was the agreed-upon date his bride-to-be was scheduled to arrive. With no other communication forthcoming, Daniel had decided to be here just in case. He didn't want his intended to show up at the station with no one to greet her.

The singsong melody of hammering and sawing echoed in the air. To his left, a new hotel was being built. To his right, a young man painted the horse rail of the general store a bright white. A wagon full of neatly cut two by fours stacked high rolled by. These were the signs of progress. The town was still lacking a few things, including a decent barber, a skilled blacksmith, and a dependable doctor. No sooner than he'd formed the thought, he saw Doc Thompson stumble out of the saloon. Dressed in a seer-sucker suit, the town physician shielded his eyes against the bright sunshine. Daniel shook his head in disgust. He couldn't abide drunkenness.

"Hello...Mis...tah Webster," Doc slurred.

Daniel tipped his hat. "Doc." He used the term loosely. He couldn't remember the last time he'd actually seen the man perform any medical miracles.

"Hotter...than Hades outh...here, huh?"

That was the one thing they could agree on. It was defi-nitely a scorcher today, yet here he sat in a buttoned up jacket waiting on a train that was already late.

"What're you...waiting on?" Doc asked.

"The train."

Daniel didn't offer any more details. What he was doing was none of the good doctor's business. As the man shuffled off, Daniel released a relieved breath. He hadn't wanted to talk to anyone about his new bride. In truth, he was kind of nervous.

What if the woman wasn't to his liking? What if she was

plain? What if she had a surly disposition? He hadn't given Mr. Potts a physical description of the one he was looking for. He simply told him to choose a woman from a good family with good breeding. His nieces and nephews needed all the help they could get. He had no time for schooling them and teaching them the proper manners. Heck, he didn't even have all the proper manners himself. How was he going to teach them? His father was no better. Sure, Levi Webster had lived the life of a respectable gentleman in Philadelphia, but without his wife's constant prodding and with no social invitations to accept, his manners had dried up like a grape in the sun.

Maybe Daniel's new bride could teach the entire family a thing or two. He wiped his damp palms on his jeans as a new thought occurred. What would she think of him? Would she find him attractive? Caroline once told him he had eyes the color of moss in summer. Sounded nice, but moss was like a fungus. Was that how she saw him? As a fungus? He shook his head, clearing thoughts of the past. Just once, he'd like to go one day without thinking of her.

He would focus on his bride-to-be instead. Based on the letter from Leonard Potts, the woman would be a young widow. He could handle that. More than likely, she knew her duty in the bedroom since she'd been married before. He was easy to please in that way. He'd had his share of floozies and loose woman when he was younger. After hours spent on the trail driving cattle, all he'd wanted was a warm bath and a willing female.

That was before he settled down. Before he became a dedicated uncle and businessman. He was focused now. And there was no better way to stay focused than to get a wife. Sure, he wouldn't have what his parents had — true love. True love had kicked him in the teeth and laughed in his face. Nope. Love had no place in his life. This marriage was a business arrangement, pure and simple. He hadn't shared any of that information with Leonard Potts. With the hefty fee the lawyer was getting, he knew better than to ask a lot of questions.

In the distance, the whistle of a train screeched. Billowing puffs of white smoke puffed in the air as the massive steel horse came into view. The time for second-guessing was over. His bride-to-be had arrived.

HAZEL ALIGHTED FROM THE TRAIN, nearly choking at the scorching temperature. She was accustomed to the humid air in Charleston. This was a dry, arid heat. She clutched her oversized, floral tapestry bag. She'd managed to grab it from the boarding house before she left Charleston. Her mama made it, and it was the only thing she had left from her. She shook the wrinkles from the full skirts of her gray muslin dress. Thank goodness, she had no money for a corset. If she'd been wearing one, she was certain the combination of the tight bindings and the stifling heat would have made her faint.

All things considered, she had no cause for complaint. Her journey had gone better than she'd expected. She'd enjoyed a comfortable ride with paid passage. Thanks to the Civil Rights Act enacted last year, segregated rail cars were no longer allowed. Even so, the few colored folks on the train still clustered together near the rear train cars.

Neither the grating of the iron wheels on the tracks, nor the showers of ash and cinders from the wood-burning loco-motive bothered her. She was so happy to be embarking on a new life. The train had stopped once per day on the five-day journey. At each stop, she'd considered getting off, but she couldn't bring herself to do it. By taking this ticket, she'd entered into an unspoken contract. She had to complete the trip. She couldn't steal Daniel Webster's money and leave him empty-handed. He expected a bride, and she was going to deliver.

Stepping onto the wooden platform, she nearly collided with a Chinese worker hauling a canvas bundle marked 'laundry.' A raven colored, plaited ponytail draped over one of his shoulders. Dressed from head to toe in black, he seemed regal and mysterious. She hadn't seen many Orientals in South Carolina. His eyes widened in astonishment. Apparently, he was just as surprised to see her as she was to see him.

"Pardon me," she said.

The man bowed slightly and then continued on his way.

Her eyes flitted across the colorful scenery surrounding the depot. She'd expected a few shabby buildings scattered amidst the tumbleweeds and sand. She never dreamed a western frontier town would have a post office, a mill, a livery, a bakery, a dressmaker's shop, and what appeared to be the makings of a grand hotel. Redemption was a sprawling town. She was impressed by its progress.

She fiddled with the lace ties of her straw bonnet. She'd like nothing better than to remove it, but she had to look like a respectable lady for her new husband. Her heart hammered. She couldn't believe she was actually doing this. She had no business here. She didn't know anything about working on a ranch. What if her new husband needed someone with experience? What if he worked her from sunup 'til sundown? What if he was cruel and mean-spirited? Or ugly? Or lame? He might even be sick, with a contagious disease like consumption. That was it! Something had to be wrong with the man. Why else would he have sent for a wife almost two thousand miles away? Why couldn't he find a willing female who lived in Redemption?

Even as she formed the thought she knew the answer. In South Carolina, the scars of slavery had left a toll. Because of the war, women and widows outnumbered men five to one. But in the west, the tables were turned. The further from Charleston she traveled, the more the population of women dwindled. That was another reason she hadn't gotten off the train when it pulled into each new station. The men ogled her like a piece of prime meat. She feared for her safety. It was obvious these prairie towns were in desperate need of females. Few women were willing to travel to the wild unknown. She was one of the brave ones— and lucky to have a wealthy rancher to sponsor her trip.

"All aboard!"

The train began to pull off. This was the moment of truth. There was no turning back now. As the engine chugged and the whistle blew, she spotted a tall, broad-shouldered man standing beside a wagon. His gray cowboy hat and tobacco-colored boots contrasted sharply with his suit jacket. He looked slightly uncomfortable, holding a bouquet of wildflowers. But even from a distance, she could see he had a kind face. Maybe he could help her.

Back home, a mutual friend or chaperone facilitated proper introductions between a man and a woman. That was before the war. Now, the measure of civility was left up to individuals.

She approached the man. "Excuse me. Do you know a man named Daniel Webster?"

Dark, wavy locks peeped beneath the brim of his hat. "You're looking at him."

Hazel brazenly allowed her gaze to roam his angular

features. A deep cleft parted his chin. His long, aquiline nose tapered into broad nostrils. When her eyes met his, moss-green orbs flecked with gold streaks openly stared back at her.

*This is Daniel Webster? He's not so bad. Easy on the eyes, too. Yes, he'll do quite nicely!*

"I'm Hazel Young." She managed a shy smile. "I got your information from Mr. Leonard Potts."

The man's jaw dropped. "Mr. Potts sent you?"

She bit her lip. Mr. Potts hadn't exactly sent her. She didn't want to lie, so she practiced the script she'd rehearsed every day since she'd boarded the train. "He provided me with your letter. You asked him to find you a wife."

"There must be some mistake." He shook his head. "I asked for...I wanted...you're not..." He let out a long breath.

From his scrunched brows and bewildered look, it was obvious Daniel Webster was not happy to see her. And who could blame him? He was probably expecting a genteel lady with milky skin and golden hair—not someone with bronzed flesh and too many freckles on the bridge of her nose. Definitely not a colored woman.

She should leave right now and go back to — to what? The boarding house? The proprietor had told her not to return without payment for her room. She'd already begged for any job she could get. Nobody welcomed a mulatto. Her stomach churned in juices of anguish. She'd come so far, only to be rejected, yet again. She had no money and no options. She had to make this work. She had to be tough. There was no better time to start than this moment.

Summoning all the courage she could muster, her eyes met his. "There's no mistake, Mr. Webster. I'm your mail order bride."

**4**

Daniel stared at the striking woman standing before him. Everything about her reminded him of a confectioner's store. Creamy, caramel complexion. Hair like black licorice. Lips the color of strawberry penny candy. Wide eyes, a few shades darker than the maple syrup he'd eaten on his flapjacks last week. She was dressed modestly in a gray dress with black slippers. She clutched her luggage as though it held every scrap of her personal belongings. Lord, she was pretty, but what was he supposed to do with a colored woman?

He would telegram Mr. Potts immediately and demand the man make things right. He paid good money for a wife. He didn't know what crazy scheme the solicitor had cooked up, but he would not be duped into participating.

"Listen, Miss Young," he grappled for the right words, "I'm sure you're a nice lady. But I think there has been some mistake. Or rather, I don't think this is going to work."

She laced her slender fingers together and wrung her hands at her waist. "It's obvious I'm not what you expected,

Mr. Webster. And for that I'm sorry. But if you give me a chance, I ..."

"Do you know anything about working a ranch?"

"No, but I know about hard work."

"You ever do any farming?"

"No, but I'm sure I could learn."

"Ever taught school?" He knew the coloreds had their own schools with teachers who seemed qualified. Maybe she could teach his nieces and nephews a thing or two.

She hesitated. She was educated and believed she would be able to pass her knowledge along. But she didn't want to lie so shook her head. "I've never been a formal schoolteacher, but my parents were learned. They taught me to read and write. I know arithmetic and I speak a little French."

He ran a palm over his freshly shaved jaw. French? What good would that do him? She had plenty of excuses, but no experience. She was useless, as useless as the lacquered floral box his mother had brought from Philadelphia. For twenty years, it had sat in the same place on the mantle. Pretty, but it served no function.

The woman eyed him with steely determination. "I've traveled for days to be here. I've endured a stifling hot rail car by day. Darn near froze my toes off at night. Been gawked at by strange men, and snubbed by socialites. I gave up everything to come meet you, Mr. Webster. Now, before I can even shake the travel dust from my skirts, you tell me I'm not wanted." She took a deep breath. "I don't have anywhere else to go. You seem like a decent, Christian man. Could you find it in the goodness of your heart to put me up for a while until I can make other arrangements? I can cook and clean to earn my keep."

Her words punched him in the gut. A good Christian

man. If she only knew, he hadn't stepped inside a church in years. Indeed, he'd faced so many challenges, he wondered if God was playing some cruel joke on him. But he did need someone to cook and clean. In a few hours the children would be home from school. Chaos would rein. He still had plenty of work to do. So, he may as well take advantage of her offer while he could. "Okay, we'll work something out. At least until I hear back from Mr. Potts."

She rewarded him with a grateful smile. Evidently she was pleased. His heartbeat quickened. He wasn't used to pleasing women. In fact, most females he met burst into tears when they didn't get their way. He'd give her credit for not doing that.

"Allow me to help you into the wagon."

He placed the bouquet and her bag in the back of the wagon, and then turned to face her. She held her arms out at her sides. She was so slender his thumbs and middle fingers almost touched when he wrapped his hands around her tiny waist. Even beneath the fabric, he felt the warmth of her skin radiate against his fingertips. For a moment, his hands itched to travel up toward the swell of her breasts. Shocked by his thoughts, he shifted his hands, but that only made things worse. His palms resting on the curves of her hips conjured up images a man should never have of a respectable lady. He jerked his hands away, as though they'd been burned by hot coals.

Fighting his strange reaction, he grumbled aloud, "I need to stop in at the post office for a moment. I'll be right back."

He left her sitting atop the buckboard seat while he walked a few doors down to the post office. Earl, the postmaster greeted him. "Hello, Daniel. How can I help you?"

It took Daniel less than five minutes to wire Mr. Potts

and demand a new bride. "I'll be back in a few days to check for any replies," he promised Earl.

Just as he'd finished paying the postage fee to have his letter sent off, the mayor of Redemption walked in. The man removed his ten-gallon hat. Originally from New York, he liked to pretend he was a true westerner by wearing an outrageous hat and spurs with his black suit. Damn fool.

Daniel nodded. "Mayor Bradford."

"Mr. Webster, did you know there is a mulatto woman sitting in your wagon?"

"Yes, Mayor Bradford. I'm well aware."

"This town is becoming overrun with immigrants and foreigners. Pretty soon, we'll be outnumbered."

Daniel scoffed. "None of us standing in this room was born in Redemption. When you think about it, we're all immigrants."

The mayor's face reddened. "Your logic is absurd, Mr. Webster."

The postmaster spoke. "Daniel has a point."

"Aw, shut up, Earl."

Daniel left the two men squabbling as he exited the post office. Sadly, the mayor only reinforced the thinking many townsfolk had about colored people. There was no way he could marry Hazel Young. No way.

Still scowling, he reached the wagon and climbed into the seat beside his unexpected companion. "Everything all right?" he asked her.

"A man in a tall hat just walked by and gave me a look like I was stink on a shoe," she said.

"That wasn't just any man. He's the mayor."

"He wasn't very friendly. I expect more from a mayor."

Daniel grabbed the reins. "Oh, yeah? Well, we all have expectations. Sometimes, they get blown to smithereens."

She huffed. "We've already established that I'm not what you expected."

"When did you last eat?" he inquired.

"On the train. My ticket included the price of my meals."

He looked over at her as he navigated the wagon out of town, his eyes glancing from her head to toes before turning his attention back to the gravel road. "Just wondering how much help you'll be. You're rail thin. Look a mite weak to handle the type of things that need doin' around the ranch."

"What types of things?"

He stole a quick glance at her as she regarded him with suspicious eyes. He shook his head and chuckled, his mind drifting to the four unruly children at home. "To handle the challenges at the Last Chance ranch, you'll need patience and strength. I need a woman who is flexible and accommodating."

"Flexible and accommodating? What do you plan on doing to me?"

Embarrassment slithered up the back of his neck. "You don't think ... no, I didn't mean it like that." He laughed out loud. "I'm not some salacious old geezer preying on helpless women."

"I may be in an unfortunate position, but I'm far from helpless. In fact, you needn't worry about me. I'm very self-sufficient." She looked away. "And I understand what the wifely duties entail if you want to reconsider marriage after I prove my worth. I won't shrink from my responsibility."

He swallowed. She was prepared to fulfill her role in every way. Hadn't he been thinking of that very thing only moments before she disembarked the train? That was when he'd expected a young widow. This woman had him totally off-kilter.

"How far is your ranch, Mr. Webster?"

"About twenty miles west of town. By the way, I'm not a stickler for formalities, Miss Young. You can call me Daniel."

"Fine." She pressed her full lips together. "You can call me Hazel."

He tugged on the reins, signaling his mare to get moving. Like it or not, for the moment, he was stuck with Hazel.

HAZEL MARVELED AT THE GREEN, rolling hills and vibrant, lush scenery. She'd assumed a ranch out west would be a filthy dustbowl, but Daniel's land was far from it. Every-where she looked, magnificent views stole her breath. She wished she could make Montana her home, but the look of disappointment in Daniel's eyes when he saw her the first time told her that could never be. His rejection stung. The fact that she wasn't who he expected was bad enough, but when he practically tossed her onto the buckboard, she'd had to bite her lip from crying.

They'd ridden in silence for the past twenty minutes. She was certain the rancher was absorbed in his own thoughts, wondering when he would hear back from Mr. Potts. Too bad the solicitor would never reply. At some point, Daniel would learn the man was dead, and then he'd write to another lawyer for a new mail order bride. Hazel would have to cross that juncture when she came to it. For now, she had to do her best to convince Daniel to let her stay for the time being until she could come up with a plan. It would be difficult. She could not ignore her bruised ego and desire to lash out. Plus, her last few attempts at conversation had ended awkwardly.

Had her skin been fairer, her cheeks would have blushed bright pink when she suggested earlier that she would be prepared to fulfill her wifely duties in the bedroom. She didn't want to think about surrendering her body to a strange man she didn't love. But if she were to be Daniel's wife, she imagined it wouldn't be so bad. The way he held her when he touched her waist showed he could have an easy-going manner when he wanted. He might be gentle in bed. He might actually make her enjoy the act. Was the rugged rancher capable of passion?

She studied his profile. Her eyes leisurely roamed his face from his thick eyebrows to his strong chin. A tiny cut slit the smooth flesh near his jaw. He must have nicked himself shaving—trying to get gussied up for his wife-to-be. Too bad, this day hadn't turned out how he'd envisioned. She blew out a deep breath, figuring it was time to speak up. She didn't want to seem uncivilized.

"My mama used to say you can't judge a book by its cover."

"What's that supposed to mean?" he asked. " I shouldn't judge you by your cover?"

"No. That means I'm not going to judge you. For instance, I see on your exterior, a man who's hardworking. Serious. Honest. Doesn't like coloreds."

His head whipped toward her. "I never said that."

"You didn't have to. I saw it in your eyes and your expressions."

He frowned. "Instead of drawing incorrect conclusions, ask me anything. I'll give you a truthful answer."

"All right. "What kind of man are you, Daniel Webster?"

"The kind who doesn't suffer foolishness or crooks."

"Sounds fair. What do you plan on doing with me?"

"I don't rightly know, yet."

She huffed. "That is hardly a satisfactory answer."

At that moment, one of the wagon wheels hit a bump

and she was thrown against him. She gripped his arm to steady herself. Their gazes collided. His green eyes held her captive. Up close, she could see his lashes were long and feathery, almost to the point of being exquisite. His gaze slid to her lips then back up to her eyes again.

"I promised I'd be truthful, Hazel. I didn't guarantee I would satisfy you."

Heat flooded her body. She'd wager all the money in the Philadelphia mint that he was entirely capable of satisfying her every desire. She cleared her throat and scooted back to her side of the buckboard seat. She placed a hand over her wildly beating heart, flustered by her reaction to him.

Eager to change the subject, she asked, "What kind of work do you do on your ranch?"

"Raise cattle, sheep, and some elk. I employ a group of men to perform the daily tasks. A few trusted hands help me with the more important jobs."

"What sort of daily tasks?"

"Whatever needs doing. Chopping firewood, cleaning out water holes, putting up hay, harvesting oats, cleaning the bunkhouse, making a supply run. Stuff like that."

"And the big jobs? What are those?"

"Herding cattle, repairing fences and buildings, taking care of the horses, including feeding them and training them. Last night, I played nursemaid to a newborn calf. Next week, we'll take some of the herd to market. That's how I make most of my money."

"How long have you been running the Last Chance Ranch?"

"For as long as I can remember. Over the years, my brother, Mark, and me helped Pa build it into the success that it is today. Pa used to do a lot more, but last spring, a randy bull gored him in the leg. Now, I handle all the day-today operations. The injury slowed Pa down enough to make him use a cane, but his mind is still sharp—and so is his tongue."

She smiled. "Your pa sounds like a handful. I'd like to meet him."

"Be careful what you wish for."

"And Mark? Will I get to meet him too?"

Daniel sobered. "He's dead."

## 5

"I'm sorry," Hazel apologized. "How did he die? If you don't mind my asking."

"In an accident."

"My mama died in an accident, too. She was working in a building when soldiers set it afire. She never made it out alive. How did your brother die?"

"I don't like to talk about it."

She looked away. She'd shared her tragic loss with him, but he couldn't be bothered to do the same. So far, all she'd done was make him frown. They were not getting off to a good start at all. She changed tactics. "What about children? Do you plan on having any?"

"I already have four."

"Goodness!" She couldn't hide her shock. "That's quite a few. So you have been married before?"

"They're my brother's children."

"Oh, what happened to their mother?"

He cocked his head toward her, a sour look twisting the corners of his mouth. "You ask a lot of questions."

"It's the only way to learn."

"When you do get a husband one day, I don't think you're going to make a good wife."

She gasped. "Why on earth not?"

"A man doesn't like his wife asking a lot of questions." He pinned her with a serious look. "He just wants a woman who listens to what he says and keeps a clean house."

She thrust her chin in the air, thoroughly irritated with him. "Well, I suppose you're right, Daniel Webster. If that is what's required, I will definitely *not* be a good wife."

She refused to make conversation after that. If he wanted silence, she'd give it to him. A few minutes later, he pulled off the main dirt road and onto a smaller winding road. In the distance, was a two-story home with vibrant red shutters, a stucco exterior and four, white columns stretching across a long porch.

"It's beautiful!" she declared, unable to resist. She had almost forgotten that she was angry with him and giving him the silent treatment.

Daniel hopped down from the wagon. His lips twitched into an impish grin. "Wait until you see the inside."

THE INTERIOR of the house was a disaster. Daniel led Hazel to the kitchen, which was in the exact same condition as he'd left it this morning. He watched her eyes sweep across the mess. He'd wanted her to see the enormity of what she was walking into. Better to get it over with now and give her a chance to turn tail.

Her full lips pressed together. "It looks like a tornado blew through here."

"Four little tornadoes to be exact."

"The children did this?"

"They can be quite rowdy."

She picked up a cast iron skillet and grimaced at the charred remains of something unidentifiable. "You can't put the blame squarely on them without putting it on yourself, too. The Bible says spare the rod, spoil the child."

"Is that what your parents did to you?"

"I was a good child, but they disciplined me when necessary."

He peeled off his suit coat and hooked it over his shoulder. "Ma died when I was eight. Pa never had the energy to whip us. He was too busy putting up fences and wrangling cows."

"I'm sorry to hear about your mother, but your father had no excuse. Children need a firm hand. It lets them know you care."

Daniel heard the rhythm of heavy footsteps, followed by what he knew was a cane knocking against wooden stairs. "Well, you can tell Pa that yourself. Here he comes now."

As if on cue, Pa hobbled through the kitchen's back door, tugging at a red handkerchief knotted around his neck. "Those sheep are gonna be the death of me." He yanked his hat off and used it to smack the dirt from his denim overalls. A cloud of dust choked the air. "I got half a mind to make mutton soup." He looked up, startled to see Hazel. His gaze shifted to Daniel. "Didn't know you had company, son."

"Pa, this is Miss Hazel Young. Hazel, meet my father, Levi Webster."

Hazel lowered the skillet onto the stove. "Pleased to meet you, Mr. Webster."

Pa nodded at her and then addressed Daniel. "Glad to see you got us another maid."

"Um, no, Pa. Hazel is not the maid. She's..." Daniel

paused, itching with discomfort. How would he explain this? Just a few hours ago, his father had told him not to mess things up. It wasn't his fault that idiot, Leonard Potts, had sent him the wrong woman. But for some reason, Daniel wasn't ready to tell Pa about the debacle.

Hazel came to his rescue. "I'm the cook," she told Pa. "You can call me Hazel."

Pa's faded blue eyes twinkled. "I can't tell you how glad I am to have something to eat besides Skeeter's salt pork and corn pone."

"Skeeter?" she asked.

"He's one of the ranch hands," Daniel explained.

"I think I can do a whole lot better than corn pone," she promised.

Pa nodded. "Glad to have you here, Hazel. Where are you staying?"

Daniel spoke. "She'll be staying with us for a while."

"Even better!" Pa grinned like a Cheshire cat, and then dry-rubbed his hands together, staring at Hazel with appreciation.

"Well," she filled the awkward silence, "If someone can show me to my room, I'll get settled in and start on this dreadful kitchen."

Pa hobbled forward. "It'll be my pleasure, Hazel. Right this way. Up the stairs." He pointed his cane toward the staircase and let Hazel pass in front of him.

Hazel strolled out of the kitchen. Pa followed, but then peeked his head back through the doorway and whispered to Daniel, "What happened to your mail order bride?"

"She never arrived. I must have got my days mixed up."

His stomach churned with guilt over the lie. Right now, it couldn't be helped. He wasn't ready to launch into an explanation of what happened. He needed time to figure things out.

Pa nodded. "Well, good job on finding us a cook. Only problem is you'll have to beat the ranch hands off with a stick."

"Why do you say that?"

"She's the prettiest thing we've seen in years. The men will be lining up to get a good look at her. They may even come a courtin'."

"Courting? But she's colored."

Pa snorted. "You don't say."

"I just meant..."

"Doesn't matter what you meant. Women are scarce in these parts. Good-looking ladies are rarer than a snowstorm in July. She could have her pick of any fella."

"Fine," Daniel snapped. "Please show her to the guest room before she thinks we forgot about her."

Pa's brows furrowed. "What's got your spurs bent out of joint?"

"Nothing. Just got a lot of work to do and I didn't need a wasted trip into town."

Daniel released a breath of relief when Pa finally shuffled out of the kitchen. He had no call to be short with his father. It was all on account of Hazel. Daniel wasn't sure why he was so irritated at the thought of one of his ranch hands trying to court her. Maybe it was because he felt responsible for her. What was Mr. Potts thinking? He planned to send a telegraph wire to the man later today. The letter he'd posted would take time and he wanted this debacle solved sooner rather than later. Right now, he had to get to the sheepfold and save his ewes from becoming Pa's supper.

∼

HAZEL SURVEYED HER HANDIWORK. She was amazed at what she'd accomplished in a few short hours. She'd washed dishes, organized the pantry, scrubbed the windows, washed the dirty curtains, found some gingham cloth to sew a table-cloth, and swept and mopped the floor.

She retrieved Daniel's bouquet of wildflowers from her room and placed them in a mason jar on the table. Then, she wandered out back to the garden, where she found fresh herbs. She dug up a few carrots and picked some wild blackberries, too. She'd told Levi she was a great cook. That wasn't entirely true. She was still learning, but when she had access to all the ingredients she needed, creating meals was much easier. Years ago, when she and Mama were impressed into labor for the Confederate army, they were both expected to tend to the wounded soldiers in the field hospitals, as well as to cook. Sometimes, there wasn't a thing to put in the pot except potatoes and a few half-starved rabbits. Most times, all they had to eat was cold biscuits, porridge, and dried jerky.

Earlier, Levi had shown her the chicken coop. One thing she could cook well was fried chicken. She began mixing flour, butter and water for a pie crust. She heard a commotion outside, but she kept working, figuring it was only Daniel and his crew of men. She was shocked when, moments later, four disheveled children stood in the doorway of the kitchen.

She smiled at the quartet. "Hello," she addressed the oldest child. In him, she could see remnants of Daniel. These must be his brother's children.

"Who are you?" the man-child asked.

"I'm Hazel. And you are?"

"August Webster."

"Pleased to meet you, August."

"I'm June," the older girl spoke up. "What are you doing in our kitchen?"

Hazel's gaze swept over the girl from head to toe. June wore a knee-length skirt over pantalettes with boots, hardly suitable for a girl her age. She should be wearing a hoop to hold out her skirt, along with a pinafore over her dress to keep it clean. She would speak to Daniel about getting the girl some proper clothes.

"I'm your new cook," Hazel said. "Your father gave me the job today."

"We don't need no cook!" the second boy barked.

June rolled her eyes and elbowed the boy. "This is our brother, March."

Hazel nodded. "Hello, March. The correct way to speak is to say, 'We don't need *a* cook.'" She wiped her hands on a nearby dishtowel. "At any rate, I don't think it's a matter of needing a cook. Your father and grandfather *want* a cook. Since I need a job, the arrangement works out perfectly."

"Are you making a pie?" June asked. "I like pie!"

Hazel laughed. "Yes, I plan to make blackberry pie, if I can find more blackberries."

"I can help!"

"Me, too," August offered.

"I'll help eat it," March snickered.

The youngest child coughed repeatedly, without covering her mouth.

Hazel bent down and wiped a smudge from the child's face. "What's your name?"

"May."

"How long have you had that cough, May?"

"She's had it about a week," August volunteered.

"I have a remedy for that," Hazel said.

May's blonde ringlets shook vigorously. "No medicine!"

"Oh, this isn't medicine. It's magic."

The girl's sparkling, blue eyes grew wide. "Magic?"

"Yes, something my daddy taught me when I was your age." Hazel issued orders. "August, put some water on to boil. June, hand me some of those peppermint leaves by the sink. March, bring me the honey."

The children scurried to do her bidding—all except March. He was as slow as the honey he brought back from the pantry. But soon Hazel collected all the necessary fixings, including ginger and lemon. Ten minutes later, she sat a cup of peppermint tea in front of May. The child hadn't seen Hazel slip in a few shakes of black pepper. She hoped the other ingredients would mask the spicy taste. May's empty cup was proof she was right.

Her snaggletooth grin warmed Hazel from head to toe. "That was the best magic ever! Can we make some more?"

Hazel laughed. "Perhaps later. For now, you all can help me prepare supper. Then, when Uncle Daniel comes home, we'll all sit down to eat."

"He never eats with us," June complained. "He's too busy."

Hazel bit back disappointment. She was looking forward to seeing Daniel again, and showing him how well she'd done, despite his best efforts to discourage her.

After the children washed up, they helped her cook fried chicken, buttermilk biscuits, roasted carrots, fresh-squeezed lemonade, and blackberry pie. Levi arrived in time to eat, and he declared it was the best meal he'd had in over twenty years. By the end of the evening, Hazel was exhausted, but she managed to read May a story and tuck the other children into bed. Perhaps tomorrow she would teach them how to play the old piano in the parlor.

Hazel did not realize then that the children were only on their best behavior this first day because she was someone new and exotic and interesting. The days ahead would not prove to be as smooth sailing.

## 6

Hazel awoke early on her second morning, washed herself in the water she'd filled in the pitcher the previous night, got dressed and headed for the kitchen to make breakfast.

Levi was already sipping coffee at the table. He looked up as she was tying the apron around her waist and smiled. "Mornin'. Sleep well?"

"Quite well, thank you," she replied. "I see I have to be up before the sun if I'm going to have the coffee made before you rise, Mr. Webster." She smiled warmly at the older man.

"No need. I rise early by choice. It's about the only time this house is quiet," he said. "Those children can be a loud bunch."

"I thought they were delightful."

Levi raised an eyebrow. "Don't think last night was an example of what's normal around here."

As if on cue, there was a blood-curdling scream from the top of the stairs followed by the trampling of feet as May bounded into the kitchen nearly knocking Hazel off her feet.

"Make him give it back!" she screamed.

"Whoa, sweety," said Hazel as she caught the child who flung herself face first into her skirt. "Make who give what back?"

"March. He took my dolly again."

March strolled into the kitchen as if he hadn't a care in the world. With a look of feigned innocence, he handed the doll to May. "I was just fetchin' it for you, May."

But Hazel caught the smirk on his face before he was able to hide it from her.

"What's to eat?" he demanded.

"I'm preparing breakfast now," said Hazel. "Are August and June up and dressed?"

"August says he ain't goin' to school today," answered March. "And June is still sleeping."

"August *isn't* going to school," Hazel corrected.

"That's what I just told you." March rolled his eyes and sighed, looking more like an adult than the eight-year old he was.

Hazel glanced at Levi who shrugged his shoulders before focusing back on his coffee. She presumed that meant it would be up to her to wrestle the remaining two children to the breakfast table and see them off to school.

Once she returned to the kitchen and started to fry bacon and eggs in the cast iron skillet, she asked Levi, "When does Daniel usually come down to breakfast?"

Levi laughed. "Daniel's already out on the ranch."

Hazel was disappointed that she missed seeing him and regretted having not been awake earlier to see that he had a hearty breakfast before starting the day's labor. She would make amends the next morning.

June and August came to the table arguing with one another.

"Shut up!" June screamed at her brother.

August laughed, poking his sister in the arm. "Make me."

June slapped his hand away, reached over and pinched his upper arm hard, twisting the skin.

"Owww! Cut it out," he shouted. "You'll never get Adam to like you if you act like that."

"I don't care. I hate him."

"That's not what I hear."

"Shut up!"

Hazel was dumbfounded. What happened to the brood of sweet, helpful children from last night? As she glanced at Levi, he smiled, lifted his cup in a mock toast and took another sip of coffee.

THE NEXT COUPLE of days passed in much the same fashion. It was a struggle to get the two older children out of bed and dressed for school. March continued to taunt May by hiding her doll and telling her she was a baby for wanting to always have it with her.

Hazel took each child aside in turn and spent one-on-one time with them, getting to know them as individuals. What did they like. What were their fears. How did they like to spend their free time. What did they hope for in the future.

She learned that June liked a boy at school, but he treated her like one of the boys and gave his attention to a girl that wore frilly dresses. Hazel promised to take June to town to select some bright-colored fabric and sew her a new dress.

August wanted to stay home at the ranch and work

beside Daniel. He could not abide the confinement of the classroom and was constantly smacked on his knuckles by the teacher's yardstick for fidgeting.

"Why do I need an education anyway?" he asked Hazel. "I learn what I need to know by staying here and tending to the horses and ranch."

"You need to learn your arithmetic if you intend to sell cattle and not be cheated," Hazel said.

After a few more practical suggestions of how August would benefit from schooling as a future rancher, he grumbled less about going to school.

Hazel soon fell into a routine around the Last Chance Ranch. During the morning, she cooked and cleaned while the children attended school. Levi stopped by during the day to check on her and to indulge her with jokes and anecdotes about the ranch. The children kept her company during the afternoon and in the evening. She cooked supper, helped them with their homework, and gave each of them lessons in French. June was excited to be learning to play the piano, just like her mother.

Daniel was conspicuously absent. He left the house before sunup each day and didn't return until after everyone had gone to bed, Hazel included.

Each day, Levi gave a different excuse for his son: He was branding cattle, or breaking in horses, or attending some other important event. She left Daniel's food in the oven each night. She wasn't sure where he was getting his other meals. She hadn't seen hide nor hair of him in nearly five days.

One night, when the house was dark and quiet, she realized she'd forgotten to put Daniel's plate in the oven. Dressed in her long, white nightgown, she grabbed a lantern and then tiptoed down the stairs to the kitchen.

Daniel's plate was where she left it, on top of the stove, and covered with a cloth napkin. She crept over to the oven and placed the plate inside.

She yelped in surprise when the back door to the kitchen burst open. A burly man dressed in a buckskin jacket stood in the doorway. His massive arms cradled a towering stack of firewood. When he laid eyes on Hazel, the man's ebony eyes lit up. "Well, well. What do we have here?"

## 7

Daniel strode through the door behind his cowhand, José. His heart stopped when he saw Hazel standing in the middle of his kitchen. A gust of wind blew in, plastering her loose nightgown against her. He could clearly see the outline of her shapely figure through the thin material. He drank in her image like a man starved of thirst. It had been days since he'd laid eyes on her. But she hadn't been far from his thoughts. He'd purposely kept his distance. No use getting friendly when he'd already telegrammed Mr. Potts demanding a replacement bride. He hadn't heard one word back from the shyster lawyer which he found irritating.

His stormy gaze raked across Hazel's lush form, starting at her bare ankles and ending at her mass of unbound hair. The black coils hung down her back like a dark cloak. For a split second, he itched to pull it into his fists, tilt her head back, and brush his lips against her plump red lips.

"Hello Daniel," she said.

Their eyes locked. "Hazel," he growled, "what are you doing here?"

His gruff voice sounded foreign, even to him. He hadn't meant to be so short, but he was bothered by his body's reaction to her. And even more upset with the fact that she was half naked in front of one of his men.

She stammered, clearly uncomfortable. "I...um, came to put your plate in...the oven. You missed supper again."

The faint aroma of fried chicken still clung to the air.

José sniffed loudly. "Musta been some dinner, Miss...? I don't think we've been properly introduced."

"I'm Hazel Young," she said. "Mr. Webster's new cook."

"Pleasure to meet ya, Hazel. I'm José Alvarez."

Daniel didn't miss the look of appreciation in José's eyes. "Thanks for your help," he told José. "That'll be all." Daniel dumped his armful of wood into a nearby empty crate, nodding his head for José to do the same.

José complied, but lingered at the back door. "I got no plans." His gaze slid back to Hazel. "Maybe Miss Young has some work I can help with and I can earn me some of that fried chicken."

Daniel's jaw twitched with irritation. "Never knew you had a soft spot for the ladies, José."

José grinned, showing a mouthful of crowded teeth. "Trust me, when it comes to the ladies, ain't nuthin' soft on me."

Daniel shot him a warning glance. José eased out the back door without a further word. Daniel slammed it behind him.

Hazel spoke up, trying to break the tension. "It was kind of Mr. Alvarez to offer help." She tried to ignore the fact that she was inappropriately dressed for the middle of the kitchen.

Daniel snorted. "He only wanted to help himself — to

you! I know you're a greenhorn in these parts, and perhaps where you come from it is acceptable to be dressed like that. Or undressed, as the case may be. I suggest you be more careful about how you present yourself in this house when you are not in your private bedroom. Could you not see that José was trying to be fresh?"

She gasped. "What's got you so hot and bothered? You've barely said a word to me in five days and when you finally do, it's to insult me!"

His gaze traveled to her bosom. Her arms were crossed, attempting to shield herself from his prying eyes. She looked so vulnerable with her bare toes pressed against the wood floor. He had to fight the urge to pull her into his embrace. He figured any minute she would flee to the safety of her room. She surprised him by staying put, her stare defiant.

"No insult intended. But you should know better than to traipse around the house like that." His tone was not the least bit apologetic.

"You really should have been here for supper with the children," she said.

"I was busy patching the barn roof."

"May has had an awful cough since I arrived."

"I've been meaning to take her to the doctor, but ..."

"But what? You've been too busy?"

"I was about to say ..."

"I've heard plenty of four-letter-words in my life, but the one that offends me most is your use of the word, *busy*! You throw that excuse around like it's supposed to be accepted as law."

He blew out a long breath. Barely here a week, yet she was already starting to sound like his father. "I was going to say that Doc Thompson isn't always available for appointments. Let's just say he has a love affair with spirits."

She pursed her lips. "No matter. I'm taking care of May's cough. If you'd been around, you would see that it is clearing up."

"How'd you manage that?"

"Tea with pepper and honey. For a wet cough, that's the best remedy. The pepper stimulates circulation and mucus flow, and honey is a natural cough reliever."

"Where'd you learn that?"

"My parents. Daddy was a medicine man. Mama was a nurse. Her father was a doctor."

"A doctor? Why didn't you tell me you came from a good family?"

She narrowed her gaze at him. "You never asked. You made your assumptions and then discarded my feelings like an old snot rag."

"I did no such thing!" It was Daniel's turn to be defensive, but he knew she spoke the truth.

What was wrong with her? He'd tried to compliment her and she threw it back in his face?

"Now that you know I'm from a good family, you like me?"

"I never said I liked you."

The minute he uttered the words, he wished he could take them back. He had no call to be so rude, but she'd made him more agitated than a vexed hornet.

Her hot glare burned bright. "A true gentleman would've never said that."

"I never claimed to be a gentleman."

"If I'd known you were going to be so cantankerous I would have never come here."

He stepped toward her, pausing mere inches from her face. "If I'd known you were going to be a pig-headed woman who would lecture me in my own house, I'd have left you at the station."

Their civil conversation had disintegrated into verbal jabs and angry barbs. A more timid female would have flinched beneath the insult. But Hazel wasn't done yet.

"Fine then," she said. "We agree, we are not at all suited. Though Mr. Alvarez seemed to like me well enough. In fact," she smirked, "he might be the kind of man who says nice things to me, and comes home in time for supper, and isn't too busy to make sure the young girls in his charge are wearing proper dresses, or that the young boys who want nothing more than to follow in his footsteps get a proper education that will benefit them later in life."

Daniel wanted to wipe that smug smile off her lips. This woman had the nerve to reprimand him in his own home, call him cantankerous, and then taunt him about not tending to his responsibilities. He should have walked away. He should have ignored the fire burning in his belly. Instead, he grabbed her by the shoulders and crushed her lips against his.

Her welcoming mouth was like a warm spring day after the last winter frost. He delved in, needing to satisfy a craving he didn't even know he had until this moment. He'd only meant to shut her up, silence her chastising mouth, but he'd gotten caught up delivering her punishment. Now, he didn't want to stop. He brazenly explored the soft folds of her mouth, stroking her silken tongue with his. When he heard her soft mewl beneath his lips, he knew there was no turning back.

~

HAZEL'S BODY heated with desire. Earlier, she'd wondered if Daniel was a man of passion. Now she had her answer. She leaned in, accepting everything he had to offer. One moment, she'd wanted to strangle him. The next, she wanted to meld into his embrace. Their tongues waltzed slowly, in a dance as old as time.

He'd hurt her feelings by questioning her intelligence. She wasn't stupid. She recognized the spark of attraction in José's eyes. At least someone was interested in her. Daniel's constant rejection affected her more than she cared to admit. She had intentionally goaded him by pretending to be interested in his ranch hand. But she hadn't expected him to react this way. By kissing her senseless.

Surely, it was a sin to feel so good, especially in the arms of a man who was not her husband. She knew she shouldn't be kissing him in his kitchen. In the middle of the night. In her nightclothes. He must think her wanton! How could she ever hope to earn his respect by acting like a saloon girl?

She dragged her mouth from his. "I don't know what kind of woman you think I am..."

He released her. "I apologize. There is no excuse for my behavior. Except..."

"Except what?"

"Except I know you enjoyed it as much as I did."

Her breath caught. "It's time I took my leave."

She turned to go, but Daniel's voice stopped her. "By the way," he chided, "you were right. We're not suited for each other. Not suited at all."

His laughter rang in her ears as she rushed from the room.

~

DANIEL WATCHED the bronco buck wildly, trying its damnedest to shake the rider from its back. Liam, one of his best ranch hands, was breaking in the new horse. With one hand he gripped the saddle horn. With the other, he clenched a rope in his worn, leather gloves. The massive charcoal stallion, aptly named Diablo, snorted and stamped, kicking up clouds of dust. He was obviously not happy with the extra weight on his back. With an aggressive animal, a trainer had to be just as aggressive. The horse could feel the rider's energy, so it was important not to be afraid. Like humans, every horse was different, with varying personalities. Domesticating a wild animal was dangerous work, but Liam was skilled at it, and Daniel paid the brawny Scot handsomely for his troubles.

"Hold on tight, Liam!" Pa shouted, clearly enjoying himself.

Daniel stood beside his father outside the fenced corral, along with August and March, who straddled the top rung of the fence, transfixed by the action. It was Pa's idea to let the boys come watch. The old man insisted it was high time they started learning about the ranch, instead of hanging under Hazel's skirts all day.

Daniel's heart galloped to the same erotic rhythm every time he thought of his beautiful guest. A week had passed since their encounter in the kitchen. The kiss they'd shared was powerful, enjoyable, and shocking. He'd never experienced such raw emotion from a single kiss. It both excited him and scared him to death. That night, he'd wanted nothing more than to run after her, sweep her into his arms and make passionate love to her. He knew that was the one thing he shouldn't do. Hadn't he already learned passion was dangerous? He'd fallen for Caroline and she'd crushed his heart, driven a wedge between him and his brother. He vowed never to become so deeply involved again. And certainly not with a woman of a different race. Even if Daniel did allow her into his heart, what would folks say? He had his ranch to think of, and these children's futures.

He watched Liam put the mustang through its paces, leading him around the corral in circles. The horse still wanted to show who was really in control. The stallion gave Liam a hard time of it, bouncing the cowhand every few seconds. Liam's head whipped back and forth so hard, it looked as though his neck would snap. Sweat stained the back of his shirt and armpits. After about thirty minutes, he was ready to give it a rest. Daniel had seen Liam work before. He knew the man would try again tomorrow. Besides, he had plenty of time. It would take about three month to fully train the horse anyway.

Liam dismounted, a huge grin splitting his square face. Guys like him lived for the outdoors, whether it was sun, rain, or snow. Putting them to work inside a bank or hotel would be a slow death. Liam waved to the boys and they waved back. Then, he dusted off his chaps and did the one thing a cowboy should never do. He turned his back on a wild horse.

"Look out!" Daniel yelled.

Diablo raced after Liam, head down, nostrils snorting. Liam sprinted for the fence and hopped on the sturdy planks just in time. He tumbled over the top railing. The toe of his boot wedged beneath one of the slats. His body twisted left, but one of his legs twisted right. The unmistak-able snap of bone cracked in the air. Liam fell to the ground clutching his leg in pain.

Daniel leapt off the fence and raced to where Liam lay

sprawled on the ground. A jagged bone protruded from the Scot's right shin. "We have to get him to town. Now! I hope Doc Thompson is sober."

"Wait, Pa," March spoke up. "I know someone who can do a better job."

## 8

H azel stared at the gaping cut in Liam's leg. A jagged bone protruded from the mangled flesh. The patient lay on a lumpy mattress in the bunkhouse. He was pale as a sheet. Hazel wasted no time slicing away his dungarees and examining the wound. The man's exposed, bare leg was not shocking to her. She'd seen worse on the battlefields. Every time Liam moved, his wound bled more, the dark sticky fluid draining from his leg in spurts.

"It's bad," she told him. "Looks like you've got wood splinters embedded in there and some bone fragments." She stared into his tawny eyes. "I'm going to have to remove all that before I can set your leg."

A circle of men stood over her, watching her every move. She turned to the boys. "August, bring me a knife. March, fetch a sturdy board." She eyed Daniel. "I'll need whiskey, too. The stronger, the better."

Liam struggled to sit up.

"Stay still," she ordered. "You'll make it worse."

"Keep away!" his thick, Scottish brogue warned. "Dinnae want no lass cuttin' on me."

"Shut up," José told him. "Miss Young ain't gonna hurt you."

Hazel smiled at her defender. "Thank you, José." She thrust a stick into Liam's mouth. "Bite this," she instructed. "You're going to need it."

His eyes grew wide as saucers as he watched her poke the tip of the knife into the flame of a burning match.

"I thought you were a tough guy," she teased. "You can break a bronco, but you can't handle a woman's touch?"

A few of the men snickered.

Hazel worked quickly to clean Liam's wound and remove the splinters and bone fragments. She ignored his grunts of pain. She had a job to do, and she couldn't slow down. A few moments later, he passed out, but she kept working. When he woke up, he'd feel like his leg had been trampled by a herd of buffalo. She wished she had morphine to ease his pain. But out here on the ranch, medicine was indeed a luxury. Her movements were practiced and efficient as she tended to him. Twenty minutes later, she had the wound cleaned, and his leg placed in a stint, bound with clean strips from one of the men's shirts. Despite not having performed surgery in over six months, she hadn't lost her touch.

"He needs a few days' rest," she told Daniel. "For now, make him as comfortable as possible."

Daniel gazed at her with awe-filled eyes." Thank you."

She nodded. "My pleasure. I would advise him to use crutches until he can see a doctor, but something tells me he won't do it."

Levi's guffaw reverberated against the metal walls. "You're right about that."

One of the men stepped forward. When he pulled off his hat to wipe his sweaty brow, a few sprigs of grey hair fell forward. "Ma'am, in all my years, I never seen such a sight. Where'd you learn to do all that?"

March answered for her. "Patching up Reb soldiers."

"Yeah," August echoed. "Hazel and her ma were nurses during the war. They saved plenty of men from getting their arms and legs chopped off from gangrene."

The man grimaced. Hazel gave into the smile tugging at the corners of her lips. She'd shared her history with the children. She thought they'd be disgusted by the stories of blood and gore, but they'd paid rapt attention. Still, she never dreamed they'd repeat the tales to anyone.

"This was a lot easier than pulling musket balls from infected flesh." She shrugged. "I'd best get back to the house. My stew won't cook itself."

The men backed away, giving her room. She stood and ruffled March's sun-kissed hair. "You did good. Both of you boys are great assistants."

March fell in step with her, clasping her hand as she walked. "Think I could be a doctor when I grow up?" he asked.

"You can be anything you put your mind to," she said.

The other men followed her out of the bunkhouse, peppering her with more questions about her medical skills. Daniel hung back, torn between watching Hazel's retreating form and keeping an eye on a still-sleeping Liam.

Pa elbowed him. "That's a fine woman, son. She can cook, clean, and patch up men. You messed up by not marrying her."

Their gazes collided. "What are you talking about, Pa?"

"Don't figure me for stupid. You plumb lost yer mind if

you think you can fool me, boy. I know Hazel is the mail-order-bride you requested."

"How'd you know?"

"It wasn't too hard. You came back with no woman, spitting some lame excuse about getting your days mixed up. You've never gotten your days confused, especially when it comes to matters of this ranch. Plus, you never brought up the subject again. You haven't brought home a bride, so I figured Hazel had to be the one. What I don't understand is why you chose not to marry her."

"Do I really have to draw you a picture, Pa? She's colored."

"You keep saying that. She's also smart, compassionate, beautiful, and talented. I would think a man would be tripping over his shoes to have a woman like that, no matter what color her skin happens to be."

He shook his head. "What would folks say if I married a colored woman?"

His father shrugged. "You told me folks didn't care what you did as long as you were making money for this town."

"Well, the bride I wanted was supposed to be a refined lady, one who could be a proper mother for the children."

"Redemption doesn't need refined ladies. Your mother was refined, God bless her soul. Caroline was refined. Nothing wrong with that. But this town needs tough women who can weather this harsh environment and stand up to men like you and me. And those children adore her. If you'd been around to notice, you'd see how much time she's spent with them these past few weeks. May's cough is gone. March is no longer sullen. June is acting like a young lady. And Hazel is keeping August in school. Seems like a proper mother for the children to me. I don't know what kind of woman you're searching for, but Hazel is the woman you need."

Daniel blew out a tired breath. He liked sweet, docile women like Caroline had been before Mark stole her from beneath his nose. He didn't like mouthy, headstrong women who didn't know how to be quiet and listen. "Hazel has been too long without a man. She has a streak of independence longer than the Missouri River."

"Her independence matches your stubbornness."

"I don't want to hear that, Pa."

"Too bad. Ever since she got here, you've been ignoring her. Some payment for all she does for us. One day you're going to realize that just because a person has a good pedigree, don't mean nothing." He jabbed a finger at his chest. "Goodness comes from here. From the heart. Not a limb on the family tree. Now, if you're done working up excuses, you need to go talk to her. There's nothing holding you back."

HAZEL JUMPED when a loud clap of thunder boomed in the night air. She slid deeper beneath the thick quilt on her iron rail bed. This was nonsense. She was a grown woman. She wasn't the same little girl who was petrified of thunder and lightning. Perhaps the storms still haunted her because her daddy died on a night like this. She remembered that night clearly. Whips of lighting cracked the sky, and thunder rolled for hours. It felt as though the heavens were opening up to receive her daddy.

As hard rain pelted the thin glass of her bedroom window, she clutched the quilt beneath her chin, chiding herself for being so scared. The lantern she'd left atop her writing desk cast long shadows on the wall. In truth, she didn't need it. The streaks of lighting illuminated her room through the windowpane. She should get up and close the curtain. Better yet, she should get a warm glass of milk. That would help her sleep. She longed for the children's chatter to distract her, but they'd gone to bed hours ago.

She tossed the bed linens aside. The moment she stood up, she caught sight of her image in the dressing table mirror. A nest of unruly curls swirled around her head. She hadn't even bothered to brush and braid her hair. It would be a mass of kinks when she woke up if she didn't tend to it now. Picking up her brush, she dragged it through her curly locks.

One hundred strokes a day. That's what her mama had told her. She wished Mama were here now. Maybe she could tell her what to do. Give her advice on how to run this house. How to handle her passion, and how to calm her heartbeat whenever Daniel was near.

Seeing him today reminded her that she was no more secure in her position than she was almost a month ago when she'd arrived. She'd made progress with the children and with Levi. But Daniel avoided her like she had a contagious disease. It was bad enough he disliked her, but knowing how his kiss affected her, made it all the harder to be around him. Apparently, he hadn't enjoyed it as much as she had. He had mocked her afterwards and hadn't come back for more.

A knock on the door interrupted her pity party. It must be one of the children. Sometimes May couldn't sleep and the child slipped into Hazel's bed at night.

When Hazel opened the door, she came face-to-face with Daniel. Covered from head to toe in muddy clothes, he never looked more handsome than he did at this moment. His eyes locked with hers. She thought she saw something different in his intense green irises. Yearning. Need. Desire. His gaze traveled up and down her body, making her hotter than a furnace. Lord help her, she wanted him. She didn't care about the consequences.

Daniel seemed startled when she opened the door, as if he was unaware that she would be the one on the other side. Once he gathered his composure, he said, "Hazel, I'm...I... uh, I just wanted to thank you for what you did for Liam."

He'd already thanked her earlier, but she was glad to see him. "You're welcome."

"I didn't know you had such skills. You took charge and did what needed to be done. I can't believe you're not a doctor."

"That takes years of studying. And money. I know enough to get by. I can save lives, if people don't mind being tended to by a colored woman."

"I don't think you'll have any complaints from the men around here. They respect you. They like you."

"It's nice to hear that someone around here does."

Daniel furrowed his eyebrows. "What do you mean by that?"

"You've made it clear that you cannot bear to be in the same room as me. How long are we going to carry on this charade? You leaving the house before sun up and not returning until after sun down, just so you don't have to deal with me. It isn't fair to the children."

She had barely gotten the last words out when Daniel drew her into his arms and pulled her against his solid chest. He kicked the door closed behind him as he nudged them into her bedroom.

Butterflies camped out in her stomach. She knew what was coming next. Her heart thumped in anticipation. Daniel's lips descended on hers. Sweet. Warm. Welcoming.

She didn't care that he was covered in filth. Or that he smelled like musk and remnants of smoked firewood. She leaned into him and kissed him back. She purred as he slanted his mouth and delved deeper, taking full possession of her mouth. His velvety tongue stroked hers.

He shook his head and pulled away, afraid of what he might do.

"Hazel, that's the problem. I *do* like you. More than I should. More than a man has a right to." He drew her into his arms again. "I've been pushing you away because I'm afraid of what we could have together. Afraid to let my guard down. Afraid to...love again. You were right when you said I could not bear to be in the same room with you. But not for the reason you think."

He pressed his lips to hers again, hungrily, and she responded by pressing her body into his, wrapping her arms around his neck.

A knock at the door startled them. They jumped back, parted.

Without waiting for an answer, a mop of blonde curls scampered into the room. "Hazel, I'm scared of the thunder. Can I sleep with you?"

Hazel recovered her composure quickly. "Of course you can, darling."

May raced across the wooden floor to Hazel's bed, leapt onto it and dove beneath the sheets, burrowing under the piles of bed linens. The precocious girl was totally oblivious to what was going on between the two adults. "Look at me," her muffled voice came back. "I'm a prairie dog."

"Yes you are," said Daniel as he approached her and tickled her.

May giggled, her tiny mouth forming an "o" when she

noticed Daniel was in the room. "Uncle Daniel, I didn't see you!"

"That's because you were too busy being afraid."

"Tell me a story," May pleaded with Hazel. "Tell me more about Charleston, when you were little like me."

The image of Hazel putting her arm around his niece as May snuggled up to her tugged at Daniel's heartstrings. Hazel's strong and steady voice began weaving a story about her life before the Civil War. Daniel sat in the chair across from her bed, listening. He realized the children knew more about Hazel than he did.

He shook his head, marveling at the woman before him. She was great with kids. She was considerate, talented, and God-awful pretty. She made his loins heat with desire whenever he thought of her. He'd been an idiot to keep her at arm's length. He let out a long breath. Maybe it was time to do as his father suggested. Maybe it was time for him to get married.

Daniel slipped from the room, closing the door softly behind him, Hazel's soft voice receding behind him as she described the magnolia trees of Charleston to an enthralled May.

## 9

Hazel hummed along to the random clucking of the hens in the chicken coop. Reaching beneath the feathers of one plump chicken, she pulled out two eggs from its nest and tucked them into the basket hanging from her arm. She needed a lot more for what she hand in mind. Today was March's birthday. She planned on baking him a lemon pound cake dripping with the sweet glaze he loved. She wasn't an advocate of feeding the children excessive amounts of sugar, but it wasn't every day a young man turned nine years old. The poor child had already grown up without his parents. He deserved a bit of sweetness. All of the children did.

She was amazed at the changes in the children. In the time she'd been here, they'd transformed from rambunctious little terrors into well-mannered, inquisitive children. All they needed was some love and attention. She wasn't the only one showing them affection. After their encounter in her bedroom, Daniel made it a habit of having the morning meal with them as well as eating supper. For the first time in a long time, she felt part of a family.

"Hello, Miss Hazel."

She turned to find José's hulking form filling the entrance to the coop. "Hello, José."

He tipped his hat. "You're looking like a ray of sunshine on a cloudy day."

She laughed. She supposed that was his way of saying she was pretty. José had his own form of communication. "Thank you."

"I thought you might want to know that Liam is on the mend. He's even using a crutch to get around, like you suggested."

"Good. I'm flattered he listened."

"Well, not really. One of the men triple dared him that he couldn't kill a rattlesnake with one of his crutches. After that, he got kinda fond of using it. He said it didn't have a thing to do with listenin' to no lady doctor."

Hazel smiled as she pulled a few more eggs from the next nest. "I'm not a doctor, José. I never claimed to be."

"I bet you could be the first colored, female doctor in the world if you wanted."

"I might have been able to, if she didn't already exist."

"Are you shucking me?"

"Not at all. A few years ago, Rebecca Lee Crumpler was the first colored woman to receive a Doctorate of Medicine in the United States."

"She actually went to medical school? Graduated and everything?"

"Yes. She graduated from the New England Female Medical College."

"Impressive."

"Yes, she is."

"No, I meant you, Hazel. You are so smart. You know a lot."

"I pick up things here and there."

"And you're humble."

She wagged a finger at him. "Why do I get the feeling you didn't come here simply to tell me about Liam?"

He shrugged. "Because you're smart, just like I said. You're the perfect woman for me. The kind of woman I would cherish and protect."

She couldn't have been more shocked if the man grew a horn. "José..."

"Hear me out, Hazel. I know I'm not a prize. I chew tobacco. I don't go to church regular. I have a reputation for liking the ladies. But I make good money. I can provide for you. There's more to me than what's on the surface. I'm a mix of things, just like my French and Spanish heritage. *Êtes-vous surpris?*"

She gasped. "Yes, she answered his question. "Yes, I *am* surprised. I didn't know you spoke French."

"There's a lot you don't know about me. It would give me great pleasure to show you what you're missing." She took a step back, and he took a step forward. He cupped her shoulders with his big hands. "Hazel, be my wife. I'll do right by you, I swear it."

She swallowed. Of all the things she woke up expecting today, this was not one of them. She did not want to offend the man nor did she have any desire to marry him. "Um, I... we ... don't even know one another."

She was starting to feel claustrophobic in the chicken coop with José's large frame blocking the sunlight. Surely she had nothing to fear from him, but she was acutely aware that they were a distance from the house with no one else nearby.

"I'd like to court you, Hazel." He rocked back and forth nervously, his eagerness obvious. "Please don't say no."

Hazel had a sixth sense that she should get back to the safety of the house as quickly as possible without riling the man up.

"This is all so sudden José," she said. "I need to get back to the kitchen now. I've already lit the fire in the stove." She was able to indicate with her body language that he should retreat from the doorway. When they exited the coop, Hazel drew in a deep breath of fresh air in relief.

José walked beside her like a little puppy dog as she made her way back to the house. She knew Levi was home so felt safe enough as she got closer to the house. She stopped at the bottom of the porch stairs to signal to José that he wasn't to follow her any further.

"Thank you for walking me back, José. I'll see myself inside and I would imagine you also have work to see to." She held her breath hoping he would take his leave quickly without any more declarations of love.

He took the basket of eggs from her hands and set it on the ground before taking both her delicate hands in his large calloused paws. "I know you need time to think about it, Miss Hazel. I'll come by tomorrow and maybe we can go for a horseback ride and plan a future together." Before she had time to react, he leaned in and kissed her on the cheek, then turned and walked briskly away.

Hazel exhaled and stooped down to retrieve her basket of eggs. She would have to find a way to let José down easy without insulting the man.

~

DANIEL WAS HEADED BACK to the house early. It was March's birthday and he wanted it to be special for the child. Hazel had promised to make a cake so they could celebrate after dinner and Levi had purchased a new saddle for the boy as a gift from the entire family.

Family.

It did feel like they were becoming a family now. The children were much better behaved and thriving. The house was spotless, they all had clean clothes and linens and there was a nutritious, hot meal on the table every night.

And he owed it all to Hazel. He had grown more fond of her each day, and was ready to commit to marriage. That was, until he ran into Mayor Bradford in town.

"You still got that mulatto woman staying with you?" the mayor asked Daniel.

"Yes, I do."

"When do you s'pose she'll be leaving Redemption?"

"Don't know, Mayor. Not sure that she will be leaving," Daniel said. "You got a problem with that?"

Mayor Bradford rubbed his chin. "It might be best if she found a bigger city to settle down in, don't you think? Someplace where there are more of her own kind."

"What makes you say that?"

"Some of the mother's of the school children where your young'uns go to school are not real happy about some of her methods." The mayor was clearly uncomfortable with the conversation. "Say she's a kind of witch doctor. Doc Thompson ain't so happy either. He's threatening to move on after he heard she tended to Liam's broken leg rather than bringing him in."

"Doc Thompson is a drunkard and doesn't deserve to keep his medical license," Daniel said.

"He's still the only doctor we have and most of us know to go see him in the morning, before he gets to drinkin' for

the day." The mayor put his foot up on Daniel's wagon
wheel and folded his arms. "It's not just for the sake of the
town and everyone here, Daniel. Think of her. What kind of
life will she have if none of the other women will have
anything to do with her? That's no life for a woman in these
parts."

When Daniel told Levi about his conversation with
Mayor Bradford, Levi was angry.

"None of his or anyone else's business," he said.

But Daniel was not so sure and did wonder what kind of
life Hazel could have in Redemption. She spent all her time
working at the ranch and tending to the needs of him, Levi
and the children. She deserved more than he could give her.

As he approached the house, he spied Hazel and José at
the bottom of the porch stairs. He would have to warn José
not to be a nuisance. He doubted that Hazel would welcome
his attention.

Until he witnessed José lean in and kiss Hazel on the
cheek. She did not appear to flinch or flee. She simply
picked up her basket and strolled into the house.

José turned away, smiling, and scampered towards
Daniel with a look of pure joy on his face.

"José?" Daniel said as the two men met on the footpath
up to the house.

"Hey, Mr. Webster."

"I don't remember assigning you any chores nearby."

"I'm way ahead of schedule, Mr. Webster. I just wanted
to see Hazel. I've declared my intentions!"

"Your intentions." Daniel's stomach tightened.

"I asked her to marry me," said José.

Daniel clenched his jaw. He needed to control himself
and not let on that José's statement had affected him. "Oh?
And what did she say?"

"She didn't say no. She said we needed to get to know each other better. I'm going to court her." With that, he skipped along the path and shouted back to Daniel, "I'll get back to my chores now!"

## 10

M arch was excited to be the center of attention at dinner and was thrilled with the new saddle. He told Hazel that his birthday cake was the best tasting cake he'd ever eaten and said the he wanted the same cake every year for his birthday.

Hazel glanced at Daniel when March had made this declaration but he would not make eye contact with her. He had been unusually sullen throughout dinner which she found disappointing for the children who could sense that something was not quite right. She was disappointed for herself as well.

She would never understand this man. One day he seemed to be loosening up, spending more time with her and the children. He would catch her gaze at inopportune moments and smile, reminding her of the kiss they shared, causing the heat to rise in her cheeks. The next moment, he was as distant as the day she'd met him and he'd told her that their arrangement was not going to work out.

Once the children had been tucked in for the night and Levi was settled by the fire with his pipe, Hazel retreated to the kitchen to wash the dinner dishes. Daniel had already withdrawn to the porch and seemed to be deep in thought.

As she was scrubbing the pots and pans, Hazel thought she heard a sound at the back door and wondered if Daniel was stretching his legs, taking a stroll around the grounds. She looked up, but did not see anyone outside the window.

She continued scrubbing with steel wool, humming to the rhythm of the back-and-forth scraping motion on the cast iron skillet.

"Gotcha!"

The arms encircled her waist and she gasped, dropping the pan in the large sink with a racket.

"José!"

José was pressed so close to her that she could barely turn around from the sink. His face was so close to hers that she could smell the mix of tobacco and whiskey on his breath, and see every stain on the few teeth that formed his gaping smile.

"I couldn't wait until tomorrow," he said. He leaned in and tried to kiss her, this time on the mouth, but she managed to raise her arms in front of her chest to hold him off.

"José, move away." Her voice was stern, determined. She was no longer concerned with offending the man. She would make it clear for once and for all that she had no intention of marrying him.

"I can make you happy, Hazel, I know it," he said, each puff of stale breath causing her to gag. "Say you'll marry me."

"She can't marry you," Daniel barked. "She's already promised to someone."

Hazel's eyes flew toward the voice behind them. Daniel

had bounded through the kitchen door from the sitting room and had José by the arm in a flash.

"Take your hands off her."

"Hey, Boss," José said. "I'm not hurting her or nothing. My intentions are honorable."

"I know what you were here for. I heard every word of it."

"Then, you know I proposed, and I'm waiting on her answer."

"I already answered for her. She can't marry you."

José nodded. "I'd like to hear the words from her pretty mouth, if you don't mind."

"She's spoken for," Daniel growled.

"Who's she promised to? You didn't say anything about that earlier today when I told you I had proposed to her."

"Gentlemen…" Hazel protested.

Daniel stared directly into her eyes. She saw a thousand words in those eyes. She saw desire, and hope, and affection and longing. She also saw protection and caring and appreciation and, dare she think, love?

He spoke softly ow. "He needs an answer, Hazel. From you."

"José, I am spoken for."

The disappointment in his eyes was palpable. She felt sorry for him, but she also felt uncomfortable by his actions. She hoped he would accept her answer and not cause any trouble going forward.

José looked from Hazel to Daniel and knew instantly that there was no hope for him. He slunk out of the back door without another word and without looking back.

Once he had left, Hazel and Daniel stood still, staring at one another for a long time without a word. Finally, she spoke first.

"Thank you for arriving when you did. I was worried that I would not be able to fend him off."

"Perhaps you should not have encouraged him earlier."

She gasped. "How dare you suggest that I encouraged that man?"

"He told me that you wanted to get to know him better and had agreed he could court you."

"And you believed him?" she asked. "Is that why you were so boorish at dinner tonight. Poor March had looked forward all day to his birthday dinner and you couldn't even give him that."

"Are we really going to talk about the children?" he asked. "Isn't there something more important that we should discuss?"

Hazel froze. Her mind went back over the last half hour there in the kitchen. The conversation between José and Daniel. She and José. The unspoken words between her and Daniel.

Daniel had told José that she was already spoken for, and she had confirmed that to him. But wasn't that only to let José down easy? To get him out of the picture?

She and Daniel and shared a look, but did he want things to go back to how they had been, with her as his cook, as nanny to the children? Or did he want more?

She waited. This time he would have to speak first.

"Hazel, you have stirred so many emotions in me that I never knew existed. I once thought I knew what love was, but now that I've met you, I don't think I really knew before now."

Her heart slammed in her chest. "Are you saying you love me?"

"Yes, I do. And if you'll have me after everything I've put you through, I would like you to be my wife."

Daniel stared into Hazel's sable eyes. He could get lost in those eyes. He could go to sleep looking into them each night, and wake up staring at them every morning.

He dipped his head low and pressed his lips to hers. He threaded his fingers through the tangled strands of her hair, and tugged on the hair at the nape of her neck. Her head fell back, allowing him uninhibited access to the long column of her neck. He nibbled the delectable skin of her throat, her ears, and her collarbone.

He returned his lips to hers and she responded by parting her lips and allowing his tongue to tease her with featherlight touches. He ached for more but she still had not answered his question.

"Would that be a yes?" he asked.

She laughed and wrapped her arms around his neck. "Yes! It is a yes."

He wrapped his arms around her slender waist and lifted her high in the air with a yelp. As she slid to the floor, still held tight in his strong arms, his mouth ravaged hers again, dazing her with a soul-stirring kiss.

"I hope this means there's going to finally be a wedding."

Levi had shuffled into the kitchen and now looked on with approval. Both Hazel and Daniel looked at him with wide grins, flushed faces, and nodded.

"'Bout time," he said, and shuffled back to the sitting room.

DANIEL PAID for the bolts of fabric stacked high on the counter of the general store. So far, he hadn't got much work done on the ranch today, but it was worth it to see Hazel happy. She'd convinced him to buy material for the girls'

dresses. She was right. They did need proper clothing. He'd been so busy lamenting his own problems, he'd sorely neglected all of the children. While he and Hazel were in town, she insisted he pick up a few books for the boys, as well.

"Mr. Webster, did you want me to load these for you?"

"No thanks," Daniel almost laughed at the proprietor, Mr. Evans. The old man was twice his age. Daniel would feel ridiculous letting him do all the work. He watched as Mr. Evans wrapped the bolts in brown paper, and then counted back his change.

"Thank you, kindly, Mr. Webster. Come back and see us again."

"Will do."

Daniel piled the stack in his arms and headed outside, running smack into Tom Cooper, owner of the town's only barbershop.

"'Scuse me, Daniel," Tom said, passing a hand through his thick red hair. "I rushed in here because I saw your wagon outside. Who's that colored woman sitting in the buckboard?"

Daniel bristled. He'd never had any problems with Tom in the past. In fact, he liked him, but at the moment, he didn't care for the man's tone. "Her name is Hazel Young. She's staying with us at the ranch."

"I didn't see her come into town."

"She arrived on the train about six weeks ago. She's my cook and the children's nanny."

It was on Daniel's tongue to say something else, to announce Hazel as his fiancée. But they had not yet spoken to the children to tell them that he and Hazel were getting married, and he wanted to do so before their school friends heard it from their parents and passed the news through the school. News like this would run like wildfire.

"It's fine to have her around the house," Tom continued, "cooking and taking care of the young'uns. But I heard those colored women can really satisfy a man. And that one's a pretty-looking thing. She might end up in a family way by one of your ranch hands."

"Watch your mouth," Daniel threatened. "Hazel Young is a fine a woman as ever walked this earth. I aim to make her my wife."

Tom's jaw dropped. "Are you crazy?"

"Crazy enough to drop you where you stand if you don't get outta my way."

Tom moved aside, but narrowed his eyes at Daniel. "You do a lot for this town. You bring in a lot of money, and supply a lot of beef. But you can't think folks will abide you being married to a mulatto. Nobody will do business with you."

"Regardless of what they think, they *will* treat her with respect when she comes into town. Or they'll answer to me." Daniel walked out of the store into the bright sunshine where his wagon was parked out front. He ignored Hazel's smiling face as he tossed the fabric into the back of the buckboard.

Tom shadowed Daniel, and pointed an accusing finger at Hazel. "That woman must be putting some powerful loving on you for you to throw away your future!"

Daniel swung around and punched the man square in the jaw. He hadn't meant to let Tom Cooper get him all riled up, but the man's comments about Hazel were uncalled for. He'd warned him that he wouldn't stand for any disrespect —and he meant it.

The barber crumpled to the muddy ground, clutching his jaw.

Hazel shot up from her seat. "Oh, my goodness! What is going on?"

"Sit down, Hazel, please!" Daniel snapped. He jumped up on the wagon and grabbed the reins. He'd had just about enough of this town and its bigoted residents.

"We can't simply leave. You just punched a man."

"He insulted you! I was protecting your honor. Now, are you going to sit down or not?"

Her full lips scrunched into a scowl. She scrambled out of the wagon, darn near tripping over her full skirts. "I'll walk."

He jumped down. "You can't walk, Hazel. What is wrong with you, woman?"

He stalked after her, easily catching up to her in front of the post office. He clapped a hand on her shoulder and whirled her around. "Hazel!"

Unshed tears glistened in her eyes. "This isn't going to work. Don't you see that? I will never be accepted here and you will end up resenting me for it."

"No, you're wrong. I love you and we are meant for one another. If I have to defend you to the entire town or to the ends of the earth, I will."

"You can't fight everyone, Daniel."

"I'm willing to try," he smiled, trying to lighten the atmosphere.

Truth be told, Tom Cooper's reaction had shaken him. Would a mixed race couple really be accepted in this town? Would he have to move? Pack up the children? His father built the ranch. It would kill him to give it up.

"Mr. Webster," a familiar voice called, "I've been looking for you."

Reverend Olsen approached with a woman by his side. Her blonde hair was curled and elegantly piled on top of her head, covered by an elaborate bonnet. Her fashionable, pink taffeta dress, edged with black piping seemed out of place in this dusty town. A white, toy poodle nestled in her arms. A pink dog collar ringed its neck.

"Reverend, what can I do for you?" Daniel asked.

"It's what I can do for you, young man. Are you ready to get married?"

Daniel's breath hitched. "How'd you know?"

"Your bride-to-be told me."

The blonde woman smiled at Daniel. Her vivid blue eyes locked with his. "I'm Claire Stanton-Montgomery. Your mail order bride."

## 11

Hazel fought to maintain control of her raging heartbeat. Standing before her was the type of woman Daniel should be with. Pale. Pretty. Blonde. Refined. Hazel scanned the woman's fine clothing. She rarely saw ladies dressed like her. High neckline, wide pagoda sleeves, and enough hoops and crinolines to make a wagon cover. No doubt, Miss Claire Stanton-Montgomery was from a well-to-do family, just as Daniel had originally requested. How could she ever hope to compete with this? Hazel couldn't decide if she wanted to cry or scream.

"Mr. Potts met with an untimely death," the woman explained to Daniel. "However, he had a partner named Nathan Greene. He's the one who received your telegram requesting a new bride. Sadly, my husband passed away two years ago. When Mr. Greene approached me with an opportunity for a new life, I eagerly accepted. So, here I am, ready to become your wife."

Hazel turned to Daniel. "It seems your worries are over. I'm sure the good people of Redemption will embrace your new wife. I just wish you had told me you had arranged for a new bride rather than allowing me to make a fool of myself."

The look of pain in Daniel's eyes crushed Hazel to her core, but she couldn't stop the scathing words from escaping her mouth. She'd let down her guard with him, given him her heart, and he still didn't want her. It was just too painful to fathom.

"Hazel, you don't understand...I—"

"Help!" A red-faced young man, arms waving frantically, ran up to the small group that had formed in the square. "Please, somebody help! The mayor's been shot!"

Daniel asked, "What happened?"

"He got hit by a stray bullet."

"Where's Doc Thompson?"

"Out cold. Drunker than a skunk, slumped over a table in the saloon."

"Dear, God," the reverend murmured.

Daniel turned to Hazel. "Do you think you can help him?"

Hazel didn't miss a beat. She was already headed in the direction from which the young man had come. It didn't matter to her that the mayor was the first person in town to look down his nose at her and had probably been the one to taint the community's perception of her. She was stronger than that. And more importantly, a man's life was at stake. Her instinct to protect others outweighed everything else.

As she strode purposefully toward the injured man, she responded. "I don't think I can help him. I know I can."

HAZEL MADE a quick assessment of the mayor's unconscious body. This was the man who flashed a sour look her way when she arrived in town and made her feel unwelcome. But none of that mattered now. He was hurt and her conscience wouldn't allow her to abandon him.

"How did this happen?" she asked Mr. McGee, the saloon owner.

"Two fur trappers got into an argument playing three-card Monte. The tall one accused the short one of cheating. Next thing I know, the short fella whips out a pistol and starts shooting up the place. The mayor walked in and got hit in the chest. The sheriff took both those fools into custody."

Hazel hovered over him and rolled up her sleeves. Someone had taken the trouble to remove his suit coat and lay him on his back on the billiards table. His long legs dangled over the carved mahogany wood. A crimson pool of blood seeped from his shoulder onto the green felt. Wasting no time, she ripped his expensive shirt and eyed the angry red hole surrounded by black gunpowder. She sighed with relief.

"He didn't get shot in the chest. The bullet is lodged in his shoulder."

"Well, is he gonna live?" Mr. McGee asked.

"Luckily for those fur trappers, he will."

She made a quick incision with a scalpel. Thankfully, Daniel had the foresight to send someone to Doc Thompson's office to bring back the supplies she needed. She could improvise when necessary, but the right tools made the job so much easier.

She was trained to work quickly, but for this procedure, she needed to take her time. She could easily nick a major artery. The irony of it was not lost on her. She had the knowledge to heal, but she also had the power to kill and no one would be the wiser. God gave her this talent for a reason. She'd never had enough hatred in her heart to intentionally take someone's life.

After she patched Mayor Bradford up, she sagged into a nearby chair, keeping vigil over her patient. For the first time, she noticed she had an audience. Daniel, Miss Stanton-Montgomery, and the red-faced man sat nearby, watching her as she'd worked. McGee even shut his saloon down while she tended to the injured man.

One of the saloon girls sat a tankard of beer in front of Hazel on the table. "On the house."

Hazel stared at the foaming head of the amber liquid. "No thank you. I could use a drink of water, though."

Daniel reached for the beer. "Wouldn't want it to go to waste." He took a sip. A foam mustache formed on his upper lip. He licked it off. He was ruggedly handsome, even with beer on his mouth.

The mayor's groans brought Hazel to her feet. She was by his side in an instant, mopping the beads of sweat on his forehead. His frantic, blue eyes locked with hers. "Where am I?" he rasped.

"In the saloon. You took a bullet in the shoulder."

He nodded. "I remember now." He tried to move, but grimaced in pain. The mayor might be handsome if not for his ugly attitude toward coloreds.

"You need to relax and recuperate for a few days. I removed the bullet and put fresh bandages on you, but you'll need to change them every day for a while." She signaled to McGee. "Can some of your bouncers help the mayor to the doctor's office?"

"I can do better than that," McGee offered. "One of the girls is visiting her ma. The mayor can use her room upstairs to rest."

Mayor Bradford eyed Hazel. "You removed the bullet?"

"Yes."

Daniel stood at her elbow. "Mayor, this is Hazel Young. Before you go on raving about how you don't want a colored woman touching you, you need to know she saved your life. She could've just let you bleed to death."

The mayor's eyes grew wide. "What about Doc Thompson?"

Daniel pointed to a corner table where the town doctor lay face down. A shot glass turned on its side and a near-empty bottle of liquor rested inches from his ear.

McGee sucked in a breath of disgust. "Son of a gun is droolin' all over my table."

Mayor Bradford turned back to Hazel. "You helped me when you didn't have to."

"Yes, I did," she replied. "We all have a choice in life. I made mine."

He shook his head, a grimace on his face from the pain the movement caused. His voice was raspy and barely a whisper. "I'm sorry. I was unkind to you and I was wrong. Please accept my sincere apology."

She believed him. She'd run across plenty of liars in her life. Mayor Bradford wasn't one. He might be a bit pretentious, but the only crime he was guilty of was bad judgment. "I won't hold it against you. Now, lay back down until McGee's men come to get you." She pushed his wadded up suit coat beneath his head, giving him a makeshift pillow.

"You're a fine medical practitioner, Hazel. We could use someone with your skills. Would you consider becoming Doc Thompson's assistant?"

Daniel snorted. "Hazel has a lot more talent than playing second fiddle to some drunk doctor. She's got her hands full on the ranch."

Hazel looked at Daniel with a raised eyebrow, signaling

to him that she would make her own decisions. He shrugged sheepishly in her direction and mouthed *sorry*.

To the mayor, he said, "But I could imagine she might want to consider opening her own clinic someday. If it suits her and she thinks she has the time for it."

Hazel nodded in approval.

Feeling confident, Daniel added, "That is, after we plan our wedding."

Their eyes met. Daniel's apologetic green eyes held hers captive. He took her hands and led her to one side of the room for a private word.

"I'm sorry, Hazel. I wired Mr. Potts the first day you arrived. That was before I realized how special you are, what a caring and honorable person you are. He never answered my telegrams. I assumed I would not hear from him and eventually that was perfectly fine with me, after we got to know one another. How was I to know another woman was on her way?"

At the word *honorable*, Hazel cringed. "But she is here now, just as you ordered. You can't just ignore that."

"You're right. She's the type of woman I thought I wanted. But I can't be with her. You're the one I want."

The blonde woman had been straining to hear their conversation and gasped with indignation. "Mr. Webster, I've traveled thousands of miles to marry you."

"And we shall deal with that."

Daniel turned his attention back to Hazel and led her to a quiet corner where no one could eavesdrop on their conversation. He clasped her hands in his. "I love you, Hazel. Whatever I have to do to prove it, I will. If it means leaving Redemption, so be it. I'd gladly give up everything I have for you.

"Hazel Young, you're my bright star, my light in the darkness. I've never met a woman with more kindness or integrity than you. It's true that the first day I met you, I couldn't imagine having you in my life. Now, I can't imagine spending another day without you as my wife. Please, marry me."

Hazel's heart thundered in her ears so loud she was sure her mama could hear it in Heaven. This is what she'd wanted from the day she arrived in this town. But she could not ignore his words. He thought she was honorable. He thought she had integrity. There was something she still needed to confess. She couldn't live with the deceit any longer.

She'd known this moment would come eventually. She just never prepared for what she would say. Once again, she drew from the well of mama's good advice. She would tell the truth.

She sucked in a breath. "Daniel, there's something I never told you." He was still clasping her hands and she squeezed them tighter now for strength.

Hazel swallowed the lump of shame in her throat, and forged ahead before she lost her nerve. She told him what happened the night she found Mr. Potts stabbed outside the tavern. She revealed how, with his dying breath, the solicitor had instructed her to take the letter.

"So, I came to you filled with dishonesty," she said. "Mr. Potts did not choose me as your mail order bride. I lied to you from the moment I met you. I knew you would find out sooner or later. Then when you had no intention of marrying me anyway, I figured I could keep cooking and taking care of the children until I could figure out where I was going to go from here."

She fought back tears, as she searched his face for some sign of his emotion. "I hope you can forgive me, Daniel. I was starving. I had no money and no other options. And then," she gulped, sucking in breath to keep herself from sobbing, "I did not anticipate how I would feel about you. How difficult it would be to leave you. To leave the children, and Levi."

Daniel nodded and let go of her hands, dropping his arms to his side. "I wish you'd told me this before, Hazel. It would have saved me the time and expense of telegramming Mr. Potts. And now Miss Stanton-Montgomery is here, having endured the long journey with the belief that a husband was waiting for her at her destination."

She bowed her head in shame. "I know. And now that she is here, and made this journey with honorable intentions, and you know the truth about me, I would understand if you chose to marry her."

Daniel stood silent for a moment. "The children would be devastated."

A single tear ran down her cheek. "May I tell them goodbye?" she asked.

"No," he said, "you may not."

It felt like a punch to her gut. Worse, she felt like Daniel was punishing the children for something she had done and she would not allow it. "I *will* speak to them before I leave." Hazel glared at Daniel with dark eyes, her arms crossed in front of her in a final show of independence. "It's my responsibility to explain to them what I've done."

"You stubborn woman!" Daniel threw his hands up in the air. "You may not say good-bye to the children because you aren't going anywhere! I love you. Don't you understand that. I'm not happy that you lied to me but I understand why you did. You are the best thing that has happened to me in my life and I'm not going to lose you now."

He reached out for her and pulled her close, kissing her cheek before pulling her tightly to him in an embrace.

Stunned, Hazel could not believe her ears. Flutters of hope danced in her belly. "You still want to marry me?"

"Of course I do. You're under my skin, woman. I can't be without you. Not today. Not ever."

"Oh, Daniel." She wanted to weep, but this time with tears of joy. "But what if we have to move? To leave Redemption because you're married to me? I couldn't live with that."

"He won't have to leave!" Mayor Bradford interrupted with a sudden burst of energy from where he still lay prone on the billiard table. "I'll make damn sure of that. You're both too important to this town. And anyone who dares to complain will answer to me."

"Problem solved," Daniel told her. "Like Pa said, there's nothing standing in our way."

She grinned, her spirits buoyed by waves of happiness. "Nearly two months ago, I came here running from my past. Now, I have a bright future with a man I adore. I love you, Daniel."

"I love you too, Hazel."

## 12

T he wedding ceremony was short and simple. Everyone Daniel invited came to see him and Hazel exchange vows in Redemption's Church of Christ. All the ranch hands were dressed in their Sunday best. Evening Sun also came, bearing baskets of sweets and Indian flatbread. The two youngest Webster children sat in the front pew—amazingly, without fidgeting or arguing. This was the first time anyone had seen them so well behaved.

June stood beside Hazel in the new dress they had made together, and both August and Levi stood beside Daniel, grinning from ear to ear.

With Levi's help, the four children had done a fine job of decorating the front porch and sitting room back at the ranch. The festive home would hold all their guests during a reception after the wedding.

Even Claire Stanton-Montgomery had been invited and come. She sat a few rows back with her dog in her lap, and a fancy feathered hat perched on her head. Currently, Daniel was paying for her room at the newly finished hotel. It was the least he could do since she'd come all the way to Redemption on his account. There was a return train heading east leaving the following week and Daniel was prepared to pay for a first class ticket, but Claire was hinting that she was not quite yet ready to leave Redemption.

"There are more eligible bachelors in this small town than the whole of South Caroline," she'd said.

Hazel had offered to help her find an appropriate suitor which Daniel found amusing. He teased his bride that she wanted to be sure that Claire Stanton-Montgomery would pose no threat.

Daniel remembered what his life had been like before he met Hazel. Back then he'd often wondered if God had forsaken him. But what he'd thought was one giant curse turned out to be a blessing. Hazel had even gotten him to start going to church again. It wasn't so bad—once Reverend Olsen got past the hellfire and brimstone parts. Daniel knew he had a long way to go towards living a righteous life. Having a God-fearing woman like Hazel was a step in the right direction.

He tugged on his tie. He was more nervous than when he'd picked her up that first day almost three months ago. Only he hadn't expected someone like her to be waiting. Just like he hadn't expected this kind of love to jump up and grab hold of him.

"You'd better be good to her, or you'll have to answer to me." Levi whispered in his ear as they waited for the ceremony to begin.

"I promise, I will treat her better than I treat myself."

Levi smirked. "That ain't saying much."

He grinned. "Okay. I'll treat her better than I treat Nelly."

"That'll work."

The two men chuckled as the wedding march played.

Levi elbowed him. "Her comes yer bride."

Daniel looked up to see Hazel walking down the aisle with Mayor Bradford. She looked beautiful in the simple, white silk gown she'd made for herself with the fabric he purchased for her. Her sheer veil draped so low it almost touched the bouquet of wildflowers in her hands. They were the same as the ones he'd given her the day they met. No one could accuse him of not being romantic.

She stopped beside him, slipping her trembling hand into his. It was good to know he wasn't the only nervous one.

They both faced Reverend Olsen. "Who gives this woman to be wed?" the reverend asked.

"I do," Mayor Bradford proudly declared.

The mayor had been their biggest supporter. The man was still trying to get Hazel to open a clinic in town. Any reservations the men had about being treated by a woman quickly flew out the window when they learned how she'd saved his life.

The reverend's booming voice echoed in the church. "Will you, Hazel Onaedo Young take Daniel Ezekiel Webster as your lawful wedded husband, to have and to hold from this day forward, for better or worse, for richer or poorer, in sickness and in health, 'till death do you part?"

"I will," she answered.

"Will you, Daniel Ezekiel Webster—"

"I will," Daniel cut the man off.

A chorus of laughter rippled through the church.

Daniel placed a thin gold band on Hazel's left ring finger. Then, he clasped her hand in his. He finally had his bride to make his house a home at the Last Chance Ranch. The town of Redemption had lived up to its name in more ways than one.

Reverend Olsen nodded. "I now pronounce you man and wife. You can kiss 'er now. If you want, that is."

"Oh, I want!" said Daniel, as the congregation laughed again.

Daniel lifted Hazel's veil and stared into her shimmering, brown eyes. He claimed her lips with a searing kiss. He couldn't convey all the passion he wanted to right now, but once the reception was over, and they were finally alone tonight, he'd show her exactly how he felt.

As the guests applauded, Daniel released her and whispered, "I aim to make you the happiest woman in the world, Hazel Webster."

Her smile made his heart swell with joy. "You already have, Daniel Webster."

## THE END

# ABOUT THE AUTHOR

Cassie Malone lives in Grand Junction, Colorado with her husband and two teenage children. When she isn't shuttling her son to basketball or her daughter to dance, she writes western historical romance with inspiration from views of the Colorado National Monument from her home office window.